THE HEALING WIND

Cowgirls in Time Romance Series

A Chill Wind

Wind Beneath My Wings

Against the Wind

The Healing Wind

THE HEALING WIND

Erica Einhorn

Ralston Store Publishing
P.O. Box 1684
Prescott, Arizona 86302

ISBN 978-1-938322-27-3

Professionally and lovingly edited by:
Jennifer Hope
www.MesaVerdeMediaServices.com

Printed in the USA.

Dedicated to the one I love . . .

CHAPTER ONE

SHE SLID THE key into the lock and paused. Normally, she unlocked the office and strode in, eager to begin her day. Today, she paused to look at the door. "Katherine Leyton, Nurse Practitioner." Kat smiled, turned the key, and walked inside. No one called her Katherine, Kathy, or even Kate. Oh, wait. There was old Mrs. Cooper, eighty-seven years old but spry and sharp as a twenty-year-old, who *insisted* on calling her Kate. But everyone else called her Kat. And she was happy with that.

Kat picked up a pen and her office phone, and wrote down her messages. There were only two calls. One to cancel his nine o'clock appointment, and another to report that she felt her baby kick for the first time. Two wonderful calls! One to celebrate new life, and one that she could celebrate an extra hour of free time. It was Wednesday and not a busy week anyway. Now she could take it easy for an extra hour. She had nothing to catch up—Kat was always caught up—so she could just relax.

Leaning her chair back, Kat opened a drawer and lay her legs, crossed, on top. She laced her fingers behind her head and sighed. Ah, this was the good life. She had a job she loved and a daughter who had one more year of college before she started law school. Now she even had Zack, who was as close to a son as she would ever have. He was a good boy, and she liked him. He was enrolled at the same college as her daughter Madison, and he was doing surprisingly well for a nineteenth-century boy transplanted to the twenty-first century.

Madison and Zack were now living together. Here in the twenty-first century—which Kat was *very* grateful for. It had taken all her willpower not to explode when Madison had announced she was going to move to the nineteenth century to be with Zack. And then it had taken all of Kat's wits and determination to make it so Zack could stay here in the twenty-first century, which was what he wanted to do anyway. Kat sighed. At least that was taken care of. Her brother Ryan, her sister Jenna, and her grandmother had all moved to the nineteenth century, by way of a cave that Jenna had accidentally discovered. But Kat was pleased that her daughter was still here with her. And with all of Madison and Zack's plans, they would stay here. No worries there.

Her daughter. Even after all these years, it still felt funny coming out of her mouth. Babies having babies. That's what Kat had been when she had gotten pregnant so many years ago. Barely sixteen. Still a baby. But she was in love, and Billy had married her, and although Billy had died in the war in the middle east, everything had worked out for her. Kat had managed to bring up a baby, go to school, and become a nurse practitioner. She sighed again as she counted her many blessings.

And then the office phone rang. "Hello. This is Kat."

"Hey, Kat. You have time to talk?"

Kat smiled when she heard her sister's voice. "Hi,

Jenna. Sure. How are things in the ole west?" She loved hearing from Jenna, but Kat still couldn't figure out what she and the rest of her family found so attractive about the nineteenth century. They didn't even have flush toilets, for cryin' out loud!

"Everything's wonderful, Kat! Couldn't be better!"

"And how's that handsome sheriff of yours? Keeping the bad guys outa town?"

Jenna laughed. "Yes, Kat. He's good at doing that."

"How's Granny? I haven't seen her in more than a month."

"You really should go see her. She's thriving there! She and Edward make such a great pair! And Ryan loves his store, and he's painting more than ever." Ryan was their brother, who had moved to the nineteenth century, and bought a general store thinking that he would have plenty of time to paint, which was his passion.

"Glad everyone is doing so well. And glad that idiot doctor hasn't seen fit to kill anyone, yet. He came close with Zack." Kat held her hand up to the light and examined her fingernails. Jenna didn't normally call to chitchat, and Kat didn't know why they were doing that now.

"Um, Kat. That's why I'm calling."

Kat pulled her legs abruptly off the desk drawer, tearing her stocking, and she sat up straight. "That idiot doctor *did* kill someone?" she demanded.

"No, no, Kat. Calm down. Everyone in Red Bluff—family and non-family alike—are all alive and all fine. Actually, I have some great news for you."

Even after Jenna's reassuring comments, Kat still felt suspicious. She wasn't sure she liked where this conversation was going. "Jenna, what's going on?" Jenna laughed into the phone, a laugh that Kat perceived to be a nervous laugh, which made her feel even more uneasy.

"Kat, I told you it was good news. I'm pregnant!"

CHAPTER TWO

STARING INTO THE mirror, he scraped the straight razor across his face. One more stroke and there, all finished. He looked in the mirror and smiled. "David Mercer, you're still dang good lookin'!" he said aloud. Turning his head this way and that to make sure he was finished, he sighed, rinsed his razor in the bowl of water on the table, and walked away from the mirror. Of course no one around here called him David. Everyone called him Doc. He was fine with that. After all, he *was* the doctor. His mother had been the only one to call him David, and she was gone now. And he missed that—being called David. There was something intimate about someone calling you by your first name.

Downstairs, he heard the door open and close. Doc never locked it. You never knew when someone would need a doctor, and his place of business needed to be accommodating.

"Doc! It's me! I'll put on the coffee!"

"I'll be down in a minute."

That would be Rachel. Doc pictured her in his mind and gently shook his head. Even Rachel didn't call him

David, and they had been having coffee together nearly every morning since she became the new schoolmarm and moved in across the street from him. He smiled again at the thought of Rachel. She was a pretty thing, bright, bouncy, good company, and she made him laugh. But was he interested in her—as a woman? No, not really. Not only was she many years his junior, but— But what? Yes, what?

The truth was that he wasn't interested. He was too old to be getting involved with a woman anyway. Instead of finding someone, falling in love, getting married, and starting a family, he had chosen to take care of his sick mother. No regrets. It was his choice. And now it was too late. Plain and simple. Doc was about to start downstairs when he hesitated and held on to the railing as an image floated across his mind.

What was her name? Jenna's sister. Some animal name. Kitty? Yes, that was it. Kitty. She didn't look like a Kitty, though. Thinking about her storming into his surgery that day to tell him how to remove the bullet from the sheriff. At the time, it infuriated him. In retrospect, though, he loved that kind of fire in a woman.

But he hadn't seen her since then, and he probably never would again. She lived in the place that Zack went —wherever that was. The place where Jenna, Sarah, Ryan, and Granny all came from.

Then there was Zack, and Doc felt really bad about that. Zack had almost died. Doc knew that. But a physician can only do what a physician can do. And Doc had done his best with Zack, and it hadn't been good enough. When he found out that Sarah, the saloon owner's wife, could take Zack somewhere so Kitty (is that her name—it didn't feel right—) could cure him, Doc was silently happy, and he gladly loaned her his wagon for the trip. He could have chosen to feel embarrassed or ashamed, but he chose happy, instead. After all, a doctor's prime duty was the health of his patients, and if the health of his patient would be better served with another health professional, then so be it.

When Zack returned from wherever he had gone, pink and lively and his arm nearly healed, no one was happier than Doc. If he ever did see that woman again, he'd have to ask her what she did for Zack. Doc wasn't too proud to ask for help from someone—even if she wasn't as educated as he was. She said she was a nurse, so she had probably worked beside a doctor somewhere. There were no actual schools for nurses—and even if there were, he knew that nurses would not have the same depth of education that he had.

"Doc? You comin' down?"

Rachel's voice interrupted his reverie. "Right now." As he treaded down the stairs he realized something. Rachel came from the same place those others came from. They had never talked about it. He'd have to ask her where that was. Maybe he'd even ask about Jenna's sister. And maybe he'd do that today.

CHAPTER THREE

"OH, JENNA, YOU'RE not! Are you sure? Have you tested positive?"

"Jeez, Kat, you make it sound like ebola or something. What happened to 'Congratulations, Jenna. I'm happy for you'? Of course I'm sure."

"I'm sorry, Jenna. Congratulations! I'm happy for you. It's just that you're *there*, and that doctor doesn't even wash his hands!"

Jenna laughed, which infuriated Kat. "It's not funny, Jenna! You're not taking this seriously enough!" Then Kat relaxed back in her chair. "Oh, you'll be coming here to give birth. I see. No wonder you're not concerned."

"No, Kat, I won't be giving birth here. I'll be giving birth in the nineteenth century where I live. But you don't need to be concerned. I've been seeing an obstetrician here since I found out. He said that everything is going perfectly fine, and that I should not have any trouble giving birth at home with a midwife—which is what I told him."

"You can't be serious! You would put your life and the

8

life of your baby in the hands of that butcher?"

Jenna laughed into the phone. "Butcher? Aren't you going a little far, Kat? For a nineteenth-century doctor, I think he's pretty good. I'll have him wash his hands, though, I promise."

"Frankly, Jenna, I'm flabbergasted. What if something happens and there's a snowstorm and you can't get through? Why can't you come here to have the baby? Say . . . the entire ninth month?"

"No, Kat."

"Okay, the last two weeks before you're due. How about that? That's not unreasonable."

"No, Kat."

"And why not?"

"Because I live in the nineteenth century now. My husband lives in the nineteenth century."

"And why can't Nick be the deputy sheriff and take care of things like he does on the weekends?"

"Because Nick hasn't done that for months—not since Rawlins started acting like a real deputy sheriff again."

"Who's Rawlins?"

"You know, the guy who was a drunk."

"Oh, great. You live in a town where the doctor is a butcher and the deputy sheriff is a drunk."

"Kat, come on, stop. Doc is not a butcher, and Rawlins has been on the wagon and clean for months now. It will be all right. Just chill, okay?"

"So why can't Rawlins watch the town while you're here waiting to give birth?"

"Well," Jenna hesitated and then continued, "that's what we had been planning."

"I don't understand. What changed your mind?"

"Last night Rawlins told Josiah that he was leaving in

9

two weeks for another job."

"Why? Why is he leaving Red Bluff? And why does he have to leave now, of all times? Can't he wait a little longer?"

"He has a new job in the next town over. He's leaving because although he hasn't had a drink in months, everyone in town still considers him a drunk. He liked the appreciation that everyone showed after he helped with Sarah's rescue, and he thinks he can get that in a new town easier than he can get it in Red Bluff."

"Who's Sarah?"

"Kat, my best friend Sarah! You know!"

"Oh, Jenna. This whole situation has me so riled up that I can't think straight. Please tell me you'll reconsider."

"I'm sorry, Kat. My mind's made up. I just wanted you to know. Now, really, I need to get off the phone and get ready for my doctor's appointment."

"Wait, Jenna. One more thing."

"What?"

"How soon are you due?"

"One month. Bye."

Kat's mouth dropped open, the phone fell out of her hand, and someone opened the door to her office.

CHAPTER FOUR

THE COFFEE SMELLED delicious, and Doc squeezed Rachel's shoulder as he walked by. She smiled up at him, and he sat beside her at the kitchen table. "How's my favorite schoolmarm today?"

"I'm wonderful! I had a great day yesterday, as usual. I do love teaching, Doc. And I am so grateful that I took this job. Listen to what little Jamie Givens said yesterday . . . "

Her voice trailed off into the distance, and Doc plunged into his daydream again. He remembered when Jenna's sister—he wasn't going to think of her as Kitty anymore, because that didn't feel right—came barging through the door of his surgery. That stern look on her face, and bossing him around like she had a right to. How many women would have the audacity to do that? Not many, thought Doc, not many at all. He wasn't sure if he had ever met any. Not that he liked anyone treating him like that—he didn't. But he liked that she had never met him, yet she stood up to him in an effort to help her sister's boyfriend. Jenna hadn't married Josiah yet, back then. Jenna's sister came across like a mother bear pro-

11

tecting her young. Doc liked that. He wasn't even sure why, but he knew he liked it.

Realizing that Rachel was silent and looking at him, he nodded his head, gave a small chuckle, and said, "That was good. What else?"

"I'm planning a new project for the kids. I'm really excited about it . . . "

Her voice trailed off again, and he relived the moment that Jenna's sister came into his office, only this time, he pictured her as a giant she-bear ordering him around and growling. He suppressed an urge to laugh and changed the scene in his head. Now, they were on opposite sides of his operating table, both of them covered in blood, leaning over someone whose belly was wide open.

Rachel's voice drifted in—something about growing vegetables in water, of all things—and then drifted out again. He nodded and smiled at Rachel for good measure and returned to his daydream. They finished the operation, stitched up the person on the table, and then, of all the blasted things to happen, Doc walked around the table and hugged Jenna's sister! Where are these thoughts suddenly coming from, wondered Doc. He hadn't even seen the woman for months, had only seen her that once, and now she was suddenly consuming his thoughts. Well, he didn't like it, and he was going to put a stop to it right now! Wait. Doc decided that he *did* like it, and if he wanted to think of a woman that he had only met once, that it was his prerogative to do so.

"Doc? You're awfully spacey today." Rachel put her hand on his hand and looked at him.

"Spacey? What's spacey?"

Rachel suppressed a giggle and said, "You're off

somewhere in dreamland."

"Oh, that. Well," stumbled Doc, "I have some things on my mind, that's all. Sorry if I wasn't paying attention. Now go on about the wet vegetables."

Rachel laughed. "I finished that story five minutes ago. It's okay," she patted his hand again. "I won't hold one spacey day against you. But I need to get to school now. The kids will be showing up any minute. Thanks for the coffee, and the, er, conversation." She laughed again, set her cup and saucer on the wooden cupboard that served as a counter, turned, and walked out the door.

Doc sat at the table for a minute shaking his head at his own rudeness when a thought occurred to him. He jumped up and ran out the door after Rachel. She was already halfway across the street. "Rachel! Rachel!" She turned and looked at him in surprise. "Rachel, what's the name of Jenna's sister?"

"Jenna's sister?"

"Yes. Jenna has a sister, doesn't she?"

"Oh, yes, she does, but I didn't realize you had ever met her. Her name is Kat."

"Okay, thanks, Rachel. Bye. Have a good day at school." Doc waved to her and walked back through the door. Yes, that's right, Kat. He knew that Kitty didn't sound right. A woman like that was never named Kitty. Kat was perfect for her. The only other name that might be more appropriate for her was Mama Bear. He laughed to himself and was about to step back into the kitchen to have another cup of coffee when he heard his front door open.

"Doc! Doc!"

"What is it lad?"

"John Junior caught a squirrel, and it bit him! Can you

13

come out?"

"Surely he could have ridden into town with you—Sakes alive! Where in tarnation did the squirrel bite him that he can't ride a horse?"

"On the hand, Doc. But it's not the bite. He fell down, and now his eyes are closed, and he won't get up."

"Run. Now. Go to the livery and ask Ezra to get Crackle and my wagon ready!"

"Can't you ride him, Doc? It will be faster."

"I might have to bring John Junior back with me. Now, run!"

Doc hurried to the other room, grabbed his medicine bag, checked quickly inside to make sure everything was there, and ran out the door.

CHAPTER FIVE

KAT WAS BUSY for the rest of the day. After three pregnant women, two well-baby checks, a tetanus shot for a
walk-in, and a physical for the mailman, Kat's day was
complete. She still didn't understand why the mailman
insisted on coming to her for his physicals. Although she
suspected that he liked her, and this was his way to get to
know her better. But she wasn't interested and would
never get involved with a patient anyway. Not only was it
wrong legally and ethically, but for her it felt morally
wrong.

Besides, she didn't really like the guy—honestly, she
wasn't interested in anybody. What happened with Billy
had been too much for her to bear. First falling in love
with him, then accidentally getting pregnant, then marrying him, then him going off to war and never coming
home. The range of emotions was almost too much to
take. She probably would have ended it all after Billy
died—except for Madison. There was no way that she
could leave an infant all alone in the world. That didn't
seem right.

And since Billy, there hadn't been another man in her

life. Kat wouldn't let them in. She knew that was it, and she did nothing to change it—didn't want to change it. For a few years she had a crush on Nick—her brother Ryan's cute cop friend. But she knew that Nick didn't like her, and that's why she liked him—he was safe. Madison didn't like Nick because of that, but Madison didn't understand the dynamic. Nick gave Kat someone to think about without ever having to do anything about it. So it was the perfect "relationship." Or, non-relationship, she should say.

Kat straightened everything up, completed filling out all the patients' charts, locked her office, and walked the seven blocks home. She had understood her parent's need to live on the ranch outside the city. And Jenna had that need, also. But Kat liked being in the thick of the city. She liked her condo, and she liked the advantage of walking to work. And she was grateful for that. Sure, there were things about the city that were less than desirable, but Kat believed in focusing on the good. Kat was comfortable and happy with her life.

Until now! Dammit, Jenna! Why are you doing this to me? "Okay, take a breath and breathe deeply," said Kat aloud. "Jenna is not doing this to you. Jenna is doing this for herself. Now you have to figure out how to help Jenna see the correct way of thinking." Kat struggled to breathe deeply, but she was too upset. What could she do to help Jenna? Well, the answer was obvious. She'd have to take a trip to the old Red Bluff and have a good ole friendly chat with Jenna. Perhaps she'd have to include that cowboy sheriff that Jenna married, too. Josiah may be just a cowboy, but he was a smart cowboy. Maybe she could get through to him if she couldn't get through to Jenna. That was an option.

Kat's breathing eased. She felt better already now that she had figured out how to handle the situation. Reaching her condo, she walked in and flopped down on the couch. Her words to Jenna and Josiah had to be chosen carefully so as not to offend them, but so they could see reason. It was essential that Jenna have her baby here and not in the nineteenth century.

She'd go Friday. Oh! She remembered that she had one appointment in the morning. She'd call him tomorrow and see if she could reschedule. It shouldn't be a problem. And with Jenna in her eighth month of pregnancy, every day made a difference. She had to get to the old Red Bluff as soon as she could.

Sleeping fitfully through the night, Kat awakened Thursday remembering broken dreams of Jenna giving birth while Kat and that stupid doctor from the old Red Bluff delivered the baby. No! She couldn't let that happen. And since too many people had scheduled appointments for the day, there was no way she could reschedule all of them. It would have to wait one more day. Then she'd leave early in the morning, convince Jenna by noon, and get her back here by late afternoon. Piece of cake.

CHAPTER SIX

ON THE WAY there, with Crackle barreling down the rough country road, Doc tried to go over all the possibilities in his head. He thought that John Junior had only fainted, and if so, he would have already recovered by the time Doc arrived. But it could be more serious. It could be shock—it could be several bad things. Doc had to hope for the best and prepare for the worst. That's what it was like being a country doctor: every house call was different, and you never knew what to expect. That's what he liked about it, really.

When he had gotten out of medical school, he had stayed in the city. But he knew right away that it wasn't what he wanted. He wanted the variety and responsibility of being a country doctor. Sure, it could be inconvenient at times. There were more nights that someone had awakened him than he cared to remember. It was always worth it, though, and he never resented any interruptions. Doc had chosen this field, and those interruptions were part of it. And he embraced every one.

He gently tugged on the reins, and Crackle eased to a stop. Doc jumped out of the wagon, grabbed his medicine bag, and was headed to the house when he saw John Junior in the doorway, braced on one side by his mother.

Doc walked to the door and gently put his hand on John Junior's shoulder. "Let's get him back into bed. He shouldn't be up and around after an experience like that —he needs to rest."

They all walked into the house, and his mother helped John Junior into bed. After fishing his stethoscope out of his medicine bag, he pulled up the boy's shirt and listened to his heart. It was more rapid than normal, but he expected that. "I think you'll be fine, John. Let's look at the bite now."

John held up his left hand, and it had a dirty rag wrapped around it. Doc removed the rag and examined the wound. There were two puncture marks just behind the thumbnail. And two on the opposing side. He could see that all of them had bled, but the bleeding had stopped now. The bites were too small to need stitches. "It looks fine. Why did the animal bite you, John?"

"Well, sir, I grabbed it by the tail and started swinging it around. When I stopped, it folded over itself and sunk its teeth right into my thumb!"

"Sounds like you deserved it, doesn't it?"

"Yes, sir. I won't do it again, sir. It hurt! And I fell down and scared Mama. I won't do it again!"

Doc looked at the boy's mother. "Do you have another cloth that we can wrap this bite in? One that you've just washed, perhaps?" He didn't know why he would even ask such a thing. A dirty bandage seemed to him to be as good as a clean one, but he had been thinking of Kat so much, and he knew that she would have insisted on a clean bandage.

The woman handed him a clean towel, and Doc wrapped it around the wound and patted the boy on the forehead. "You stay away from those squirrels now, you hear!"

"Yes, sir."

"Thanks, Doc, for coming out. What do we owe you?"

"He was already up and fine when I got here. Seems to me that you don't owe me anything."

"Oh, but Doc, you had to come all the way out here. I baked a pie yesterday. There's half left. Would you take that? Please?"

Doc smiled at the woman and nodded. "Thank you." He took the pie, which smelled delicious, and put it and his medicine bag in the back of the wagon. Then he scratched Crackle behind his long ears, whispered to him, stroked his neck, and climbed into the wagon seat for the ride home.

Crackle knew the way, so Doc sat in the seat, holding the reins loosely, and daydreamed his way back into town. He wondered again at why he would even ask for a clean cloth. It seemed stupid, useless, but somehow he felt good that he had done it. And he knew that Kat would approve.

CHAPTER SEVEN

KAT ARRIVED EARLIER than usual at the office and immediately called the gentleman who had an appointment
Friday morning. He resisted an appointment for the
following week, but he finally agreed to come in that day
if he didn't have to wait too long. Kat did it gladly. She
put him in before a woman who always came in late.
This man always arrived early. So she would just take
him first, he wouldn't have to wait, and everyone would
be happy.

Friday's were always light days for her. She tried to
keep them completely free, but if someone really needed
to get in, she always let them. To walk the seven blocks to
the office for a quick half hour appointment was no big
deal for her. Kat rarely left town, but that was exactly
what she was going to do this week. If going back in time
a hundred years to the same town you lived in counted.
She thought it did. So she was glad that the one now-
rescheduled appointment had been the only one she had
to deal with.

Thursday was packed with appointments, almost back
to back. It was all she could do to take a quick bathroom

break before her next client walked in. She'd have to order in just to have anything at all to eat for lunch. That was okay, though. There was a health food store down the street that delivered. She could have an organic greens salad, sweet potato fries, and a grass-fed hamburger on a gluten-free bun. Perfect.

Kat's business thrived. She was a much in-demand nurse practitioner. That was because she was efficient, accurate in her diagnoses, and good at listening to people's complaints. She never cut people off from explaining their issues and never presumed that she knew more about them than they knew. It was their bodies, after all. And although Kat treated everyone with kindness, there was a drill-sergeant type feel about her. That didn't seem to matter, though, her days were almost all booked. Granny said that it was because she was a smart cookie. Well, thought Kat, she was, but she didn't think that's why people kept coming to her. Kat thought it was because she listened to them and considered what they said—and she didn't think that many other health professionals did that—with the exception of veterinarians, maybe.

And so Kat's day rapidly sped by. When she finally caught her breath from dealing with one patient after another, it was time to go home. Kat sighed, walked to her door and locked it, and then flopped back into her office chair. After a day like this, she felt she had to unwind before heading home. She took a few minutes to breathe deeply and try to meditate on nothing. In her youth, when she had first started her own practice, she had experimented with taking her blood pressure before meditating and after, and it was always lower afterward. So she always took time to relax after a hard day. Sometimes she'd wait until she got home, but after a particularly hard day with one patient after another and barely a breather in between, she did her deep breathing right at the office. That way, she could feel almost refreshed when she arrived home.

After several minutes of relaxing and resting her brain, she set to work cleaning the office and updating all the charts for the day. It took her longer than she expected, and when she finished she was all tense again. Ten quiet minutes and much deep breathing and meditating later, she felt okay. But before she walked home, she wanted to make a phone call.

"Hello."

"Hi, Madison. How are you? How's school?"

"Everything's great, Mom. I'm still keeping my grades up—even with Zack here. That's what you were really asking, right?"

Kat gritted her teeth. Why was Madison always so defensive with her? Perhaps it was because Kat had run her family like she ran her business—like a drill sergeant. Too much discipline and not enough love. Well, there was plenty of love—showing that love wasn't one of her strong suits, though. "No, Madison. I knew you would keep your grades up. I was wondering if you were having *fun*."

"Oh, sorry. Yeah, I have more fun since Zack's here. He's as studious as I am, so we fit together perfectly."

"Madison, I have no doubt you do. If I hadn't thought that, I wouldn't have done what I did for him. You know that."

"Okay, Mom, point taken. Thank you for doing that. But are you going to hold it over our heads forever?"

Kat exhaled slowly and tried to calm herself. Why do

conversations with Madison always end up like this? "Madison, I'm sorry, honey. No, of course not. Why are you always so defensive with me?"

Madison was silent for several seconds. "Because you've taught me to be," she said quietly.

Kat squeezed her eyes tight shut and willed herself not to cry. Sometimes the strongest people were the most vulnerable. Madison's comment had touched Kat in a place she didn't want to be touched. Taking a deep breath and biting her lip, she managed to say, "Can I talk to Zack, please?" without breaking down. She had wanted to ask Madison more questions, but not after that comment.

"Sure, I'll get him." And without so much as a goodbye, Kat heard the phone receiver hit the table.

"Hello!"

She felt her tension melt. At least Zack wasn't defensive with her. "Hi, Zack! How's school? Are you still enjoying it as much as you thought you would?"

"It's *wonderful*, Kat! More wonderful! I can't thank you enough, Kat, for what you did for me. I'll never forget it."

"No problem, Zack. No problem. I was wondering, though, if you could do me a favor?"

"Sure, Kat. Anything."

"Can you brush and saddle Paisley for me, so I can take off early tomorrow morning?"

"Sure! Is eight o'clock early enough?"

"That would be perfect, Zack. Thank you. Can I ask you something, Zack?"

"Of course."

"Do Jenna and Josiah still visit periodically?"

"Yeah. They usually come once a week, but Jenna said

they wouldn't be staying over anymore because Rawlins quit."

"Did you know that she was pregnant?"

"You couldn't miss it! She's huge!"

"Why didn't you or Madison ever mention it to me?"

Zack's enthusiasm noticeably waned. "Jenna asked us not to. She said you'd be upset if you knew."

"Jenna was right about that. She told me yesterday, and I *am* upset." Zack stayed quiet. "Zack, doesn't Josiah realize that Jenna and the baby would be much better off if she gave birth here?"

"Josiah offered to stay here for the ninth month. He said that way he could eat ice cream every day until the baby was born! But Jenna didn't want to do that. She said her home was there now, and that's where she wanted her baby born."

"Oh. My sister is a stubborn one, isn't she?"

"You won't convince her."

"What . . . ?"

"That's where you're going on Paisley tomorrow, right? To the old Red Bluff to persuade Jenna to come here? She won't do it. She's made up her mind."

"All I can do is try, Zack. All I can do is try."

CHAPTER EIGHT

THURSDAY MORNING DURING coffee, Doc and Rachel had an animated discussion on the advantages and disadvantages of public schooling versus home-schooling. They agreed on almost everything and came to the conclusion that any education was better than no education at all. Feeling guilty about his lack of attention to her the previous day, Doc gave Rachel his rapt attention. Then she left for school, leaving Doc finishing his last sips of coffee and going over their conversation in his head.

Doc had been surprised that Rachel had gone to college. And surprisingly, Rachel had been surprised that Doc had gone to college. She said that she didn't think "doctors did it that-a-way in the nineteenth century." Whatever that meant. Occasionally, Rachel would say something that shocked him, surprised him, or that he would wonder about later. Her comments about the nineteenth century always made him wonder. It was almost like she was from somewhere else where the time was different. But how could that possibly be?

He remembered back to when Josiah got shot and Kat

had brazenly told Doc that she was from the future—as if it was true! Doc laughed and furrowed his brow. Wait. Josiah had said that both Jenna and Kat were from the future and so were those two men who were with them. But Josiah was drunk at the time, wasn't he? Was he? The whole idea was preposterous! And washing your hands before surgery was, too. He thought back to the day before when he asked for a clean rag for John Junior's hand—why had he done that? Well, it was common sense, of course. If you had an open wound, you wouldn't want dirt getting in there, would you? It wasn't anything that he had ever thought of before. But he would give it some thought now.

He took another sip of coffee, blinked his eyes, and raced upstairs. A stray memory had crossed his mind, and he wanted to see if what he remembered was true. Rummaging through the big roll-top desk, Doc shuffled through everything, strewing papers and letters about, until he found what he was looking for. It was a letter from a schoolmate chum of his who now worked in a hospital in Boston. He read the letter over and then read it again. "Sakes alive! The dang woman is ahead of her time!"

One more time he read over his friend's words and let them sink in. Some surgeons at the hospital were adopting a new practice before surgery. They would clean wounds *and* clean their instruments in carbolic acid. His friend claimed that it reduced infections after surgery. Dang. Doc had to find out if he could get some carbolic acid, and then he'd give it a try. He smiled and rubbed his hands together at the thought of another way to help people.

It was after nine o'clock, and no one had come in. A

slow day. Doc liked slow days, because it meant that he was keeping people healthy. Then he realized what he needed to do today. Something he had been meaning to do and had been putting off. Go see Josiah's wife, Jenna. Kat's sister. Normally, when a first time mother became pregnant, she would rush to him as soon as they realized it. Jenna never had. He had noticed that she and Josiah disappeared a couple of days each week, and Doc thought that maybe they were returning to where Jenna came from to see a doctor there. Or maybe Kat was taking care of Jenna's pregnancy. Regardless, Doc was the medical professional in this town, and it was his responsibility to make her feel comfortable. He'd ride out there after lunch.

CHAPTER NINE

DOC SPENT THE morning going through all his books and searching for any information related to carbolic acid. He wanted to know more—especially since he felt it was one small thing that he and Kat now had in common. Well, not exactly in common, but it did make him feel closer to her just knowing about carbolic acid. When he re-read the letter for the fortieth time, he noticed that his friend never mentioned the surgeons washing their hands. But with this new development, anything was possible.

Then he walked over to Ralston General Store to see about ordering some. As he approached the store, he realized something. Ryan was Jenna's brother—which meant he was Kat's brother, as well. Hmmmm. Perhaps now was the time to act. Although, Doc reminded himself, he hadn't seen Kat since that first time, and there was a chance that he would never see her again. No matter. It wouldn't hurt to ask.

"Good morning, Ryan." Doc closed the door behind him and strode toward the counter.

"Morning, Doc. How are you today?"

"Doing great, I dare say. And you, Ryan?"

"Great, as usual. Look at my newest painting!" Ryan pointed behind him to a large landscape behind the counter.

The colors were beautiful, and Doc recognized the area as that around Josiah and Jenna's ranch. "That is a beautiful painting, Ryan. When are you going to start selling them? That one would look wonderful in my surgery. It would give my patients something to look at while I poke at them with my instruments!"

Ryan laughed. "I'm not ready to part with any yet, Doc. They're still just for me, right now. Maybe later, though— How can I help you?"

"You probably don't have any in stock, but could you order some carbolic acid for me?"

Ryan frowned. "Carbolic acid."

"It's for medical purposes. I just read about it."

"Oh, okay. I know where to look then." Ryan dragged out a catalog from under the counter and began leafing through it. "It might take me a while to find it, though."

"Okay. Order some for me when you find it. Thanks!" Doc turned to go, but after putting his hand on the door knob, he turned back around to Ryan. "Hey, your sister, Kat . . . is she married?"

Ryan gave a quick glance upwards to Doc and then returned to the pages of the catalog. "Not now, Doc. She's a widow."

Doc closed the door quietly behind him. As he walked back to his office, he thought maybe that explained why Kat was a little on the stern side. A woman alone had to be. He didn't know why, but knowing that about Kat made him like her even more—like she was vulnerable and needed his help. Laughing to himself at that thought, he entered his office. That woman didn't need help from anybody. She was tough, that woman. Tough.

After eating lunch, Doc moseyed over to the livery, gathered a couple of brushes, and walked into Crackle's stall. When the big animal nuzzled him, Doc pulled a wilted apple from his pocket. "You knew I'd bring you something, didn't you, big guy?" Doc gently rubbed the long, smooth ears, and ran his hand along Crackle's neck. "What a good boy, you are, Crackle!"

"Hallo, Doc. You want a saddle today, or should I get the harness?" Ezra ran the livery and often saddled or harnessed Crackle if Doc was in a hurry.

"Just a saddle today, Ezra, thanks."

A minute later, Ezra had swung a saddle and saddle blanket up on the stall gate. "Here ya go, Doc. Have a good ride."

"Thanks, Ezra. Would you take these for me, please?" Doc handed him the two brushes and pulled the saddle blanket off the gate. After placing the saddle blanket on Crackle's back, he put the saddle on and tightened the cinch. Ezra had left the bridle on the gatepost, and Doc slid the bit into Crackle's mouth and put the headstall on over the big ears.

After climbing into the saddle, Doc urged Crackle forward. When they turned the corner to head out of town to Josiah and Jenna's ranch, something occurred to him. Maybe they were in town. He turned Crackle around and rode back to the sheriff's office. He hopped off, tied the bridle loosely to the hitching post, and stepped inside. Rawlins sat behind the desk.

"Hallo, Rawlins. Josiah here?"

"Naw, he's enjoying his last few days at his ranch."

"What d'ya mean?"

"Didn't you hear? I'm leaving town. I've been dry for months now, but everybody still thinks of me as the town drunk. Time for a change!"

"You're right, Rawlins. Thats a hard image to live down. You've made a remarkable recovery, though. I give you a lot of credit for that."

"I got myself a new job as a deputy in the next town over." Rawlins motioned to the west with his chin. "They don't know me there, so I can make a fresh start."

"I wish you all the luck in the world, Rawlins. Good luck to you, man!" Doc gave the man's hand a firm shake, turned around, and walked out the door.

Back on the trail, Doc looked around and enjoyed the slow, quiet ride. Often, like the other day with John Junior, his rides to a patient's home required speed. He was looking at this as a pleasant social visit. It was not like he was interested in getting more business. This was his standard pregnant woman speech. And if Jenna wanted to go elsewhere to have her baby, then that was fine with him, too.

Before he was ready to give up his peaceful ride, the ranch came into view. They had done some upgrading to the property, and it looked good. Doc wrapped the reins around the new hitching post in front of the house and knocked on the door.

Josiah opened the door and smiled. "Come on in, Doc! We've been meaning to come talk to you. We're glad you're here." Then, turning his head toward the inside of the house, he said, "Jenna! Doc's here! Come on out!"

"Hallo, Josiah."

Jenna waddled up from a back bedroom. Doc couldn't believe how big she looked—like she could give birth any minute. He'd seen her in town, but he hadn't seen her lately. Maybe she'd give birth right now while he was there, and it would save them all some trouble!

"Hallo, Jenna. Nice to see you."

"Come on in, Doc, and sit down." Jenna walked farther into the house, and Josiah eased her onto the sofa and then sat beside her.

Doc sat across from them and smiled. "You look very pregnant, Jenna—in case you didn't know."

Josiah and Jenna laughed. "We've been meaning to come talk to you, Doc. Jenna's been seeing another doctor in, er, another town, but she wants to give birth here." Josiah patted her leg affectionately.

"Well, you don't have to worry about a thing, Jenna. I've delivered hundreds of babies, and there's nothing to worry about."

"My official due date is a month from yesterday."

"Did you go to a gypsy fortuneteller?" asked Doc, with a smile.

"Oh! Yeah, well—"

"What she means, Doc," Josiah said, looking nervous, "is that she's due in about a month. That's all." He looked at Jenna.

"Well, do you mind?" Doc stepped forward with his hand out toward Jenna's belly.

"Of course not." Jenna sat up and pulled her loose blouse away.

"Hmmmm. You're not as far along as I thought. Yes, a month more is about right. Although you know how babies are—they come out when they want to come out." Doc stood up and looked at Josiah. "Let me know when her water breaks, and I'll ride out directly."

"Unless it happens really soon, we'll be in town, Doc.

Have you heard that Rawlins is leaving?"

"Yes, Josiah. I stopped by your office today. Must make it more difficult for you, but I think it's good for him. Being a drunk—tough thing to live down. Well, I better get back to town now. Good day, Jenna. Bye, Josiah."

CHAPTER TEN

KAT STOOD UP to gather her belongings before heading home. Then she sat back down. She had one last call to make. Wait. She shouldn't do this on the phone. What needed to be said, needed to be said in person. Picking up the phone, she called the number that she had memorized so many long years ago.

"Hello?"

"Hi, Nick. This is Kat."

"Oh." His voice sounded disappointed. "Hello, Kat."

"Nick, are you busy? Is there any way I can come over —very briefly—and talk to you?"

"Yeah, sure. Come on over." Nick's voice sounded like her coming over was the last thing in the world he wanted right now. But she had to give him credit. He said yes.

"Thanks, Nick. I have to walk home and get my car first, so I'll be there in fifteen minutes."

"See ya, Kat," Nick said without enthusiasm.

Kat locked the office and strolled briskly home. She didn't bother to put her belongings in her condo, she just threw them on the passenger seat and started the car. Ten minutes later, she pulled up in front of Nick's house

—the same house he had grown up in.

Sitting for a minute in the car, she closed her eyes and commanded herself to relax. Stepping from the car, she shook her body like a dog shaking off water, and then, swinging her arms like she hadn't a care in the world, she walked to his door and knocked.

Nick opened the door, greeted her unenthusiastically, and invited her in. "You look tense, Kat, what's up?"

"I can't fool you, can I?"

Nick shook his head, sat down, and motioned her into the chair across from him. "I've known you too long. You can pretend to be relaxed, but I can see how tense you are."

"Nick," she looked at him seriously, "wouldn't you like to take a month's leave of absence and be deputy sheriff of the old Red Bluff?"

"Sure I would. What happened to Rawlins, though? Is he drunk again? He was doing really well last time I stopped in there."

"No, not drunk. He's quit. Moving to another town."

"Oh, wow. So now Josiah will need another deputy." Nodding his head, Nick stood up and paced back and forth across the room.

Kat held her breath. It was going better than she could have imagined. Nick was not only thinking about it, but he seemed incredibly responsive to the whole idea.

"Yeah! I like this idea, Kat. Yeah. Thank you for telling me. I'll have to go back and talk to Josiah about it."

Kat brightened. "Oh, Nick, if you could do this, it would be great!"

Nick tilted his head, confused. "Wait. What are you talking about? And why are you telling me, anyway?"

"Oh. Jenna's pregnant."

"Yes, I know."

"You knew that Jenna was pregnant?" asked Kat. Nick nodded. "I guess everyone knew but me." She shook her head from side to side. "Anyway, I always expected that whenever she got pregnant, she would naturally come back here to have the baby. But with Rawlins leaving, Josiah can't come, and she won't come without him."

"Isn't she due soon, though? Last time I saw her she was pretty big."

"A month."

"A month! Oh, well, I could never arrange to leave here that fast, anyway. A guy is on vacation now, and two more after him. It would be probably two months before I could move there anyway."

Kat sighed. "Oh, well. It was worth a try." Kat stood up. "Thanks for listening anyway, Nick. I appreciate it."

"What are you going to do now?"

"Convince Jenna that she has to come here, regardless."

"Do you think you can convince her?"

"I have to. I just have to."

CHAPTER ELEVEN

KAT WOKE UP after a restless night's sleep. She was despondent. How would she ever persuade Jenna to come back here without Josiah having some sort of backup? She had to try. She had to maintain a positive attitude, be calm but persuasive, and gently show Jenna the error of her ways. Jenna's life could depend on it. Why didn't she see that? All the questions in the world aren't going to change things. Kat quickly dressed, had some yogurt and a green smoothie for breakfast, and drove over to Madison's house—which was Jenna's house before Jenna moved to the old Red Bluff.

After parking her car out of the way, she walked straight to the barn. As promised, Zack had brushed and saddled Paisley. Her bridle hung just outside her stall. Two minutes later, Kat and Paisley, a beautiful leopard appaloosa, were on the trail that led to the cave.

Kat didn't visit the old Red Bluff too often, though she always meant to. Her grandmother, Granny, lived there with her new husband, Edward. And Kat thought that she really should visit more often—Granny wasn't getting any younger. Then again, as cantankerous as

Granny was, she'd probably live forever.

As she rode, she went over and over the whole scenario in her head. Kat needed to approach Jenna in the gentlest way, not insist or come off as controlling. Kat was Jenna's older and wiser sister, *and* she was a health professional. Jenna should naturally listen to her. With any luck, she would.

Kat knew that gentle was the way to approach Jenna, and it would be the only thing that might work. She rehearsed the conversation in her mind until she had it perfect. This would work! So caught up in her thoughts, she didn't even realize she had come through the cave, and suddenly Jenna's ranch was up ahead. After putting Paisley into the barn and taking off her bridle, Kat strode purposefully to the front door and knocked.

When Jenna opened the door with one hand on the door frame and the other on her belly, Kat took one look at Jenna and her plastered-on smile drooped, and she said, "Jenna! You *must* have your baby in Red Bluff!"

Ignoring her, Jenna laughed and walked over to the couch and plopped onto it. "Kat, I knew you'd come here and try to do this. But no. My mind is made up. My child will be born in the old Red Bluff—where he belongs."

"Jenna, you must reconsider. Listen to reason, Sis. It's not safe here."

"I live here, Kat. My husband lives here."

"You know what I mean. What if something goes wrong? I'm not wishing anything bad on you, but I've attended hundreds of pregnancies and sometimes, something bad happens."

"It won't. I'm sure of it."

"You can't be sure. And it's your first born. Those are

often more difficult."

"You don't remember Mom's story? About how Dad got her to the hospital just as you slid your way into the world? And if I remember correctly, you had a similar experience when Madison was born. How long was your labor with Madison?"

Kat looked down. "About five minutes." Looking back up at Jenna with a pleading look in her eyes, at least she hoped it looked like a pleading look, she said, "But you don't know if that will happen to you. It might not be that easy at all."

"I'm counting on it being that easy, Kat. Besides, Josiah and I have been attending Lamaze classes."

"Lamaze? Josiah? They didn't even have Lamaze— Oh. You mean in *my* Red Bluff."

Jenna laughed. "Yes, *your* Red Bluff. Of course."

"Where is Josiah, anyway? I'd like to talk to him."

"He'll be in any minute. He's in the root cellar. But he won't listen to you. He only wants to make me happy— which is what a good husband should do!" Jenna laughed again.

"Jenna, this is serious, and all you're doing is laughing."

Josiah had come through the front door and heard the last comment. "Hi, Kat. What's serious?"

"Josiah, you must convince Jenna to have her baby in my Red Bluff."

"Kat, I tried. She's made up her mind. You think *I* can change it? Think again!" Josiah laughed.

Kat sighed, put her hands over her face, and slowly shook her head. "What can I say to persuade you to do the right thing?"

Sternly, Jenna said, "The right thing, Kat, is to have

my baby in the old Red Bluff. And the right thing for you to do is accept that. Graciously. If you can." Then, gentler, "Look, Kat. I know you want to help. But if you really want to help, then support me in my decision. Besides, Doc came out yesterday, told me that he's delivered hundreds of babies, and he assured me that everything will be all right. And it will."

"Doc? You mean that butcher who calls himself a doctor?"

Jenna frowned. "Kat. He's not a butcher and you damn well know it! After he fished that bullet out of Josiah's arm, you told him that he had done a good job. I trust him."

Kat fumed but didn't say anything. She gritted her teeth, drew her hands into tight fists, and felt her chest tighten; then a thought occurred to her. A wonderful thought. A perfect thought. She smiled, and that smile was somewhere between what might be called angelic and what might be called devilish. After a quick glance at Jenna, she looked at Josiah. Right now, he seemed the more reasonable of the two. "You know the trouble Zack had with moving to the future, Josiah? You want your child to have a choice, don't you? Sure you want him or her to live here, but if the child wishes to live in the new Red Bluff, you would want that child to have that option, wouldn't you?"

Josiah's face changed, and he stood up. "Jenna, she's right. The boy must have a choice. You have to have the baby in the new Red Bluff so he can have a proper birth certificate!"

"Boy? What boy?" asked Kat.

"My son! My son must have a choice." Turning to Jenna, "You need to listen to her, Jenna."

41

"How do you know it's going to be a boy? Have you had an ultrasound, Jenna?"

"No, Kat. Josiah just knows."

"A man knows these things," Josiah agreed.

"And Kat, no, that won't make me change my mind. I've already considered that, and after our son is born, we will take him to the doctor I've been seeing and say that I delivered at home. Period. No big deal."

"You can't possibly take him right after he's born. And if you go a few days later, the doctor will know that! And —"

"Enough, Kat. I'm not changing my mind no matter what you say. So stop trying. It's getting annoying."

"You two fight it out. I'm going back to the root cellar," said Josiah, as he walked out the front door.

"There will be no more fighting, Kat. I'm not listening to another word you have to say on the matter. You may be older, but it's my body and my baby. He'll come into this world in the nineteenth century, where he belongs."

Kat, still frustrated and fuming, stood up stiffly and without another word, walked out of the house. After she was back on Paisley and trotting down the trail, she said aloud, "Well, that didn't go well, Kat."

CHAPTER TWELVE

KAT KNEW WHAT she needed to do. She needed to tell that so-called doctor a thing or two. The nerve of him telling Jenna that everything would be all right! How could he possibly know that? What an ignorant, uneducated, arrogant jerk!

Wait! Kat had been so caught up in her anger that she wasn't watching where Paisley was going. Now, she pulled back the reins as the horse was about to enter the cave leading back to the new Red Bluff. "Where do you think you're going, young lady? Home? I don't think so! We still have some business to take care of here!" Kat moved the reins and guided Paisley back to the main trail. When she saw the sign for Red Bluff, Colorado, Kat realized there was someone she needed to talk to before addressing the good doctor.

A few minutes later, she slid off Paisley and wrapped the reins loosely around the hitching post in front of the hotel. Walking in, she saw that no one was around. Even the door to Eliza's—the one right beside the front desk that was always open—was closed. The only sound she heard was something in the restaurant. "Hallo!" she called, making sure to use the old west "hallo" instead of the present-day "hello."

"In here, granddaughter."

"Granny! How did you know it was me? I only said one word!"

"Granddaughter, I was there to hear your first word so many years ago, so I think I know your voice by now."

Kat hugged Granny. "Where is everyone?"

"Oh, they all went somewhere and left me in charge of the place. I'm just earning my keep."

"Edward, too?"

"No, that old coot is upstairs taking a nap. That way he's still fresh when he comes to bed at night!" Granny giggled and continued wiping off the tops of tables.

Ignoring her comment, Kat reached out and took Granny's hand. "Do you have a few minutes to sit down, Granny? I need to talk."

"Sure, granddaughter. Any break is a good break in my book! What's on your mind?"

"Jenna."

"Oh. You found out, did ya?"

"She told me. It's about time! She's eight months pregnant!"

Granny shrugged. "Eight comes after seven."

"Granny, this is serious. Jenna insists on having her baby here. You know it's not safe!"

"I gave birth to your mother at home, Kat. Do you know how many women have given birth at home, from the dawn of time? And even now, more and more women are choosing to give birth at home. You know that."

"And if there's a problem—"

"And if there's a problem, we will deal with that when the time comes."

"Granny, I came here thinking you would help me convince Jenna to do the right thing. But you sound like you're on her side!"

"Your side, her side. There are no sides to this battle, Kat. It's Jenna's decision. It's her body and her baby. She and Josiah decide what's right for them. You can't change that."

"Granny—" Kat was reduced to pleading now. She hated that.

Granny looked serious, or as serious as Granny ever looked. "You know what you have to do, Kat."

"Yes, I know what I have to do! I have to figure out a way to persuade Jenna to have her baby in the future. And I can't believe you're not going to help me!"

Granny made a noise that sounded like a snicker, but she kept a straight face. She put her hand to her ear. "I hear Edward calling me. Must run now. Bye." Standing up, she shrugged her shoulders and walked away leaving Kat at the table alone.

Kat felt confused. The restaurant was silent. The whole hotel was silent. No one had called Granny. And why had Granny snickered? "Oh, no!" Kat slapped her hand to the side of her head. "I must be getting old. Granny," she called out, "what did you mean when you said I knew what I had to do? You obviously didn't mean convincing Jenna." Kat rested her face in her hands. "You didn't mean—"

Granny smiled and turned to face her. "Now you're catchin' on, granddaughter. Now you're catchin' on."

Granny disappeared in the back, and Kat was left at the table all alone. Shaking her head slowly back and forth, she said quietly to herself, "There has to be another way. There has to be another way." Kat was determined to find a solution. Maybe she could kidnap Jenna back to the twenty-first century. Ah, probably not realistic.

With her frustration over not finding an immediate answer to her dilemma growing, Kat decided to focus her mind on something else instead. That so-called doctor! Her irritation at the situation fueled her anger, and by the time she walked resolutely out of the hotel, she was seething.

CHAPTER THIRTEEN

DOC HAD A frustrating morning. First, Ryan stopped by early in the morning as Rachel was leaving, to tell him that it would be a minimum of two months to get the carbolic acid. He said that in the catalog under medical supplies, it mentioned a minimum delay of two months to get it, and then it would take time to transport it to Red Bluff. Since Doc was eager to try it, this was unfortunate news. When Ryan asked what Doc needed it for, and Doc told him, Ryan had gotten a faraway look in his eyes and said that his sister Kat may be able to find something like carbolic acid that Doc could use instead —until it arrived. Doc had told him that he'd just wait instead of using anything that wasn't already proven. Ryan had shrugged his shoulders and left.

But the whole conversation had left Doc feeling all-overish. He had gotten the uncomfortable feeling that Ryan was holding something back or not telling him something. Well, whatever it was, Doc wasn't going to worry about it. There were too many other things on his mind right now.

After Ryan left, a family came in from another town.

They had been visiting relatives, and their six-year-old son had fallen out of a tree and broken his arm. It was a simple break of the humerus without the bone breaking through the skin, thank goodness. But the kid wouldn't stay still. It took both his older brothers and his father to hold him still while Doc worked. And Doc prided himself on working quickly. First he wrapped the arm in wool, and just when he had it like he needed it to be, the boy twisted out of everyone's grasp and ran to his mother who sat in the waiting room nursing a baby. His father brought him back, but then Doc had to re-apply the wool.

Then Doc cut out some pasteboard for the splint, which he put water on first so it would mold more easily to the boy's arm. After wrapping the arm in bandages, just before Doc was to make the final touch of applying a thick coat of starch to hold everything in place, the boy twisted out of their grasp again and ran to his mother. Luckily, the bandages held everything in place, so after Doc tightened them just enough, he rapidly put on the starch, put the arm in a sling, and sent them on their way before the kid could manage to come out of the splint and ruin all of his good work. He was glad they lived in another town. That kid was trouble. Let another doctor handle it. But at least they had planked down the five dollars. And cash was always good.

So after such a frustrating morning, when Doc heard his door open, he expected it to be more of the same. And when he heard the door slam, he knew he was right.

Kat came storming into the examining room with a furious look on her face. When Doc saw her, he said, "Hallo, Kat," which surprised her. Her mouth was half open about to say something, but with that, she closed it, looked at him, and then erupted into fury anew.

"You old hack! How dare you tell my sister that everything will be all right with her delivery! You know better than that! You know the risks of what might happen! I can't even call you a doctor after behavior like that! What is your first name?" she demanded.

"David." He shrugged. "And what might happen?"

"If things go awry, she might have to go to the hospital! So it's better she knows that upfront so it won't come as a surprise if it happens. You arrogant fool, David!"

Doc looked around the room but stayed silent.

"What are you looking for, David? No one is going to come to your rescue!"

"Madam, I do not need to be rescued from an irate but ignorant woman who *thinks* she knows what she's talking about. What I was looking for was a hospital. Last time I looked, there wasn't one within two hundred miles. And yes, bad things can happen during birthing. But since there is no hospital around here, isn't it better for your dear sister to believe that everything will go all right so she doesn't come into labor tense and anxious? Which as you should know, just makes everything worse."

Kat balled her hands into fists and thrust them down at her sides. "You leave my sister alone, David!"

She said his name like it was a bad word. Staying calm, Doc said, "That would be difficult, madam, since I will be the one bringing her child into this world."

Kat held up her fist and shook it. "I *hate* that! I hate that Jenna won't listen to me and come back to—" She shook her head, making her blonde curls bounce around her face. "I hate it! And I hate you, David!" With that,

49

she turned around, flung the door wide open, and without closing it, stepped through and marched down the street.

Doc walked into the waiting room to the front window to watch her go. She put the reins over her horse's head, checked the cinch, and climbed into the saddle. To her credit, she didn't kick the horse.

He shook his head and laughed aloud. "You wanted someone to call you by your first name instead of Doc! Be careful what you wish for!" He shook his head again thinking that he had something else in mind when he had thought it would be a good idea for someone to call him David. Still laughing to himself, he closed the front door and returned to his examining room to check his supplies. Well, he thought, I guess that ends my daydreams of *her*!

CHAPTER FOURTEEN

KAT FELT MISERABLE. Her trip to the old Red Bluff had been an abject failure. After all her rehearsing, she had taken one look at Jenna, and all her carefully thought out plans had fallen apart. Jenna looked ready to burst at the seams! Kat was regretful that she had acted so inappropriately that she could not ask to feel Jenna's belly. That way she would have known better where the baby was at in its development. Now, she could only guess, and her guess was the baby would be born soon. But she really didn't know. She didn't know much more than *David*—and he probably knew more because Jenna would have let him examine her.

And oh, how rudely she had acted toward David. It felt funny calling him that. Now that he had explained himself—and had sounded like a professional—it felt strangely intimate using his first name. He was right, of course. Since there was no hospital in the old Red Bluff, scaring a pregnant woman with horror stories was not a good idea. And how he remained calm as she stood there yelling at him like a screaming banshee! Kat nodded her head. Yes, she had to give him credit for that. He stood up to her, and not many men would have done that—especially when she had gone off like that—acting like an idiot, really. The whole day would have embarrassed Kat if that emotion had been something she ever experienced. But it wasn't. So she felt bad and left it at that.

After putting Paisley in her stall and giving her a good brush-down, Kat stood there with her arms around the big mare's neck. It had been a long time since she had really spent time with the horse, and it felt good. Kat had read somewhere that being around horses gave a person a sense of well-being. At that moment, she felt sure that it was true. When Paisley pulled away and grabbed a mouthful of hay from the feeder, Kat sighed, gave her one last stroke on her neck, and reluctantly walked out of the stall.

She headed toward the house, hoping that Madison and Zack would be home. Confessing what she had done was not something she had even considered; but she did think that talking to family would make her feel better. Although she had walked into that house for years without knocking, knowing the sexual habits of young people, Kat knocked. No answer. After waiting a polite amount of time, she knocked again. Finally, she turned around and saw that Zack's truck was gone, and probably the two of them with it. Zack had sure made himself comfortable with the twenty-first century!

Disappointed, Kat rambled over to her car, turned around one last time in case Madison was home and at the door, and seeing nothing, stepped into her car and drove home. She couldn't cook—she was too distraught. She couldn't read, she couldn't clean, she couldn't do anything without feeling like a heavy weight hung over her head. So she sat down on her couch with her hands in her lap and tried to clear her mind. That was an impossibility after the fool she had made of herself—first with Jenna and Josiah, and then with the doctor.

But she started breathing deeply, and finally, clarity came. She remembered what Granny had said to her. "You know what you have to do." Kat knew what Granny had meant but didn't want to face it. She *couldn't* face it. She had manipulated and cajoled to keep Madison from moving to the old Red Bluff. And now that Madison and Zack were safely ensconced in college, how could Kat possibly move there? Well, it would only be a month, maybe two if she stayed to help Jenna. She could transfer all her clients to someone else for the time she was away. If they decided not to return, it would hurt business, but Kat had been thinking of cutting her practice down, anyway.

If she did move back there, temporarily, she might get to know that doctor better. His actions impressed her, and she would like to know more about him. Not that she liked him as a man, of course—just a professional colleague. Kat decided that as a peace measure, when she returned to Red Bluff, she would bring him some medical books. She'd go to the book store the following day. When she gave him the books, he would know *when* she came from; but she didn't see any harm in that. Updated medical procedures would help everyone in that town. And her family lived in that town. And she loved them. And if she had to admit it, she missed them, too.

CHAPTER FIFTEEN

DOC HAD A quiet Saturday, and Sunday morning was as peaceful as ever. He had spent most of the morning reading his old medical textbooks. They were not easy to come by, and even when he ordered them, he was never sure if they would ever arrive. But he enjoyed reading the newer ones and learning about new techniques and discoveries, and he could even learn from the old ones. When he was alone, and he often was, he spent his most blissful time reading.

Kat's outburst in his office hadn't dampened his enthusiasm for her, though. He was not about to hang up his fiddle just because she had yelled at him. He not only loved her fire, but when those blonde curls were bouncing as she was shaking her fist at him—well, all he could think to do was hug her. He hadn't, of course. But he thought that a hug was what that woman sincerely needed. And if he ran across her again, whether she was storming at him or not, a hug was exactly what he was going to give her. Just what the doctor ordered! Doc laughed at his own joke.

Just after one o'clock, Doc ambled over to the hotel

restaurant to eat. He didn't like to go right at noon, because too many people might be there, and he wanted to avoid that. When Doc received chickens, eggs, or the occasional lamb for payment, he would give them to Eliza and Samuel at the hotel, and they would keep a tab for him. Then he would go over there for most of his meals, and they would subtract it from his tab. It worked perfectly for all concerned. Their restaurant was busy enough that none of the food went to waste, and he always had nutritious meals. If he had to cook for himself, he wouldn't eat nearly as well. When his mother was alive, she did all the cooking—until she got sick—and then he filled in. But that was the two of them. With just him, cooking wasn't as enjoyable as it used to be.

When he had first made arrangements with Eliza and Samuel, random people would interrupt his meals constantly. Whenever someone came into the restaurant and saw him, they would remember some little complaint they had been meaning to ask him about. He had never seen so many odd bumps, sprained fingers, bilious attacks, and hangnails as when he ate in the main restaurant. People, realizing he was there every day, had even started coming in the restaurant just to see him. It became like his second office. He could not get through a meal without at least one interruption.

When Doc couldn't take it anymore, Eliza had someone bring him a plateful of food to his office. That change of pace stopped the constant interruptions. But finally, Samuel had fixed a table for him in the back of the restaurant just inside the door to the kitchen. No one saw him, and no one knew where he was. And fortunately, no one interrupted him. As he sat there, watching the food preparations in the kitchen and eating some delicious meat loaf, he thought about how lucky he was to live in a town like Red Bluff. Everything about it was wonderful, perfect. He might have been stuck in that hospital in Philadelphia, treating strangers and never getting to know his patients. No, he liked it right here.

Then his mind wandered again to Kat. He wished that she would come to Red Bluff more often so he could get to know her better. While Doc wasn't exactly sure of what his kind of woman might be like, he thought that maybe Kat came close to it. She was knowledgeable about medicine, so they had that in common, but she was also strong-willed, and he liked that, too.

Doc knew that he was strong. In his youth when he had taken young ladies out while he attended college, he would often overwhelm them with his strong nature. One woman that he had dated, whose nickname was Shushu, would agree with every word out of his mouth. She was a pretty little thing, with a lively personality, similar to Rachel, but one day he decided to test her. Doc had pointed to the sky and said, "Look. The sky is green today." Shushu had nodded her head and said, "Yes, Davey, the sky is green." That had been the end of that. Kat would never go along with anything like that.

Doc heard a crash and someone yell, "Oww! Oh, drat it all!" As Doc turned around to see what was going on, Samuel yelled, "Doc! We need you here now!"

Doc jumped up and ran to the area behind the big oven. There was Granny, with Edward and Samuel holding her up. A large bowl had fallen to the floor and broken, and one piece of glass had made a large cut in Granny's calf. Blood poured out. "Get me some clean towels!" said Doc, as he kneeled beside Granny. Samuel brought him the towels, and Doc held one firmly on the cut trying to stanch the flow of blood.

"What's going on in here?" Josiah came in from the restaurant. "Oh, Granny! Will she be okay, Doc?"

"I think she'll be fine, Josiah, but we need to get her to my office. Can you help carry her? I need to hold this on her leg while we walk."

"Sure, Doc. Let's go."

"I can walk!" said Granny. "No one needs to help me. I'm perfectly capable of walking across the street on my own."

"Granny, you *will* allow us to carry you across the street. It is *not* an option! I need to control the bleeding, and it will be difficult enough with them carrying you. So just relax and let us do this. Samuel, Josiah, you carry her, yes, like that. Edward, hold her hand and comfort her. Yes, thank you. Granny, I'm going to hold this on your leg. Try to stay still."

"Oh, tarnation! There's nothing wrong with me that a good whiskey won't cure!" said Granny.

They walked out of the hotel with Eliza holding the door for them. Jenna held Granny's other hand as they walked. Outside, Zack had just dismounted from his paint horse. "Zack!" called Josiah. "Go get Kat now! Granny's hurt!"

Zack swung back on his horse in one easy motion. "You got it, Josiah!" And he sped off down the street.

CHAPTER SIXTEEN

KAT HAD A fabulous morning. Now that she had recon-
ciled herself with *temporarily* moving to the old Red Bluff,
she was finding all kinds of reasons to be happy about it.
The day before, she had gone to two book stores to get
the best medical books that she thought Doc would
enjoy. They sat in a backpack by the front door so she
wouldn't forget them.

After returning from the book store, she had called
two nurse practitioner colleagues and an obstetrician
friend, had explained to them that she had a pressing
matter to attend to in which she needed to be away from
Red Bluff for a couple of months, and would they mind
taking a few of her patients for her. All three had readily
agreed. She still needed to take care of Monday's appointments, reschedule with her colleagues the remaining appointments for the week, and then call all her
other clients to inform them that she would be unreachable for two months. Unreachable—a hundred years in
the past—unreachable was putting it mildly!

She had one large bag packed and had other clothes
strewn on the bed ready to place in the backpack. Then

she had cooked and eaten a delicious grass-fed beef meatloaf with fresh parsley and red pepper, fresh organic asparagus, and a delicious green salad. Relaxing on the couch and smiling, Kat felt like she was at peace with the situation. She accepted it, embraced it, and looked forward to it—especially the part about getting to know the doctor better—but she kept that pushed to the outer recesses of her mind because it felt so foreign to her.

The phone rang. Kat sighed and leisurely walked over to it, answering on the third ring. "Hello."

"Kat! Granny's hurt! You need to come now!" said an agitated voice that she recognized as Zack.

"Where are you calling from, Zack?"

"I just came through the cave. I'm calling from my cell."

"Do you know where Josiah caught the rustler? That spot by the road?"

"Yes."

"I'll be there in ten minutes! Can I borrow your horse?"

"If you can ride bareback—"

A brief second passed while Kat controlled her urge to tell Zack when she started riding bareback. Instead, she just said, "See you in ten. Bye." She hung up the phone before hearing Zack say good-bye, grabbed her medical kit, stuffed it into the backpack by the door, and raced out to her car.

Seven minutes later, she jumped out of the car, handed Zack her car keys, and jumped on Echo's back. Zack handed her the backpack.

"You can run him, but make him walk through the cave," said Zack.

"I know how to treat a horse, Zack. But thank you. I'll

take care of him." And she sped off.

The horse was fast—much faster than her old mare—though Kat couldn't even remember when she had last run Paisley. She pulled him up at the entrance to the cave, walked through it, and Echo took off again without urging when they came out the other side. She stopped the horse in front of Doc's office, slid off, and dropped the reins over the hitching post.

When she walked into the office, Jenna and Josiah were sitting in the waiting room quietly talking. Edward was pacing back and forth. When Jenna saw Kat, she said, "She's in there. Doc made us wait out here."

As Kat approached the examining room door, she heard Doc say, "I told you, nobody in my—oh, it's you, Kat. Come on in."

Kat looked over the situation. Granny was sitting placidly on the table with Doc stitching her calf. "Wait!" said Kat.

"Oh, let him finish, granddaughter. I made him wash his hands and sterilize the needle. He's doing fine. Hardly hurts at all. Ow!"

Doc smiled at Kat and resumed stitching. Kat dropped the backpack against the wall and stood by Granny. She looked at the wound. It was six inches long, and a little blood still seeped out. Doc's stitches were even and perfect. She could not have done a better job herself.

"Oh, I should ask if you would like to finish, Kat." He held out the needle to her.

"Oh, just finish what you're doing, Doc, before I use my good leg to kick you in the bum! Just get it over with!"   Granny folded her arms across her chest and glared at him.

"Go on, Doc. You've done a great job," said Kat.

He resumed stitching until he finished. "All done, Granny. You'll be good as new in no time."

"Get me off this dratted table, then."

"Not so fast. I still need to bandage the wound to keep it clean." He turned around and opened a windowed cabinet on the wall.

"Doc, I have some fresh, clean bandages that you can use." Kat knelt by her backpack, unzipped it, reached in, took out her medical kit, and removed a package of fresh bandages. "Here. You can do the honors." She handed him the bandages, replaced the medical kit back inside, and then re-zipped the backpack.

Doc took the package from her, and she saw him furrow his brows at the sight and feel of the cellophane wrapping. "I'm not even going to ask," he said, as he pulled the bandages from the package.

Granny chuckled. "You have a thing or two to learn about my granddaughter, there, Doc."

Doc looked up, met Kat's eyes, said, "I'd like to," and then started wrapping Granny's leg.

When he finished, he helped Granny off the table and said, "You need to stay off that leg for a while, Granny. It needs time to heal."

"Doc," she said seriously, "you know what happens to someone my age who hangs out in bed all day? They never get out of bed, and they die there! If you think I'm going to lay around all day while life goes on around me —"

"Whoa, Granny, whoa. Just take it easy. No working for a while. I didn't say anything about staying in bed all day. Just don't work. And try to keep the leg elevated."

"Oh, well, get my husband in here." Louder, she said,

"Edward! What are you doing out there playing hooky when your wife almost lost her leg? Get your butt in here and help me home!"

Edward came in with a sly smile. "Oh! It's you! I thought you had died and gone to heaven so I could move on and find myself a younger woman."

Granny laughed, and they hugged. Then Josiah came in, and he and Edward helped Granny out the door.

"Kat, thanks for coming," said Jenna. "We didn't know how bad it was, but Doc took care of everything."

"He did a great job for Granny, Jenna. I couldn't have done any better myself."

"Well, thank you, Kat. Coming from you, that means a lot." Doc nodded his head at her.

Kat looked at him, not sure if that was a compliment or an insult, but she let it go. "Jenna, let me help you back to the hotel."

"I don't need help, Kat. Just walk with me."

They were about to go out the door when Kat turned around to Doc, who was wiping down his examining table. "Doc, there are some books in that backpack that I brought for you. Go ahead and take a look at them."

CHAPTER SEVENTEEN

"You brought him books? From the future?" asked Jenna.

Kat smiled and shrugged. "I decided it wouldn't hurt anything if he knew. And the whole town—including my family—will benefit from his 'updated' knowledge."

Jenna tilted her head and looked at her sister. "*That's* a new attitude, Kat. You gave me the impression a couple of days ago that you thought he was incompetent."

Kat frowned and exhaled sharply. "Well, I went to see him after talking to you and screamed at him and acted like an idiot. And he was so calm and self-assured that he impressed me."

"He was very good with Granny—didn't put up with any of her crap, but listened to her when she *suggested* that he wash his hands and sterilize the needle—and he worked quickly and made her feel at ease. And he even asked for clean towels to put on her wound when it first happened!"

Kat's eyes lit up. "Really? So he's learning, then. That's good."

"You looked at his work. Were the stitches properly

done?"

Kat shook her head from side to side. "He did a great job. I wasn't exaggerating when I said I couldn't have done any better myself. Very skilled with his hands." She shrugged again. "I was impressed."

They had reached the saloon and were about to cross the street over to the hotel, when Kat turned her head and looked down the street the way they had come. "Oh, no! Zack's horse! He's gone!"

"Where did you leave him?" asked Jenna.

"I dropped the reins over the hitching post in front of Doc's office. Zack's going to kill me."

Jenna took Kat's arm in hers and began walking across the street. "I'm sure he's fine, Kat. He probably just walked back to the livery where he used to live."

"I should go check!" She started pulling her arm out of Jenna's and then hesitated. "Oh, I should check on Granny first—make sure that cantankerous old woman isn't dancing a jig or anything. With Granny, there's no telling what she might be up to."

Jenna nodded. "That's for sure."

Kat opened the door to the hotel, and Jenna walked in first. They heard commotion in the restaurant and headed in that direction.

"I said stop hovering! I got cut! I'm not dying! Now everybody let me be!" growled Granny. The group of people standing over Granny slowly moved away, and Kat saw Granny sitting at a table with her bandaged leg stretched out in front of her on a chair. Kat walked over and put her arm around Granny's shoulders.

"Granny? Are you all right?"

"I'm fine, granddaughter. That doctor did a bang-up job. He even washed his hands without protest! But you should have seen the look on his face when I asked him to do that! I tell ya, granddaughter, that was worth the injury right there! He's a good man, Kat. It wouldn't hurt you any to get to know him better, if you know what I mean."

Kat pulled away, and Jenna stepped up to Granny and squeezed her hand. "Hi, Granny. I'm glad you're all right."

"That husband of yours, Jenna, is a good man. I'd keep him if I were you."

Just then, Edward walked up to the table and put a cup of tea in front of Granny. "Your tea, milady," he said and bowed his head.

Granny chuckled. "See, I told you he treated me like a queen. Thank you, husband of mine."

Edward looked at Granny's leg and grimaced. "I'm worried about you, old woman." He ran his fingers lightly over the bandages where a little blood had seeped through.

Kat looked at the bandage and nodded her head. "It's all right, Edward. A little seepage is normal. Doc did a good job."

Edward sighed, blew a kiss to Granny, and walked away. A commotion at the front door drew everyone's attention.

"What now, I wonder." said Granny. "Do you suppose Jesse James has come to town or something?"

Kat smiled as she saw who had come through the door. Madison rushed in with Zack at her heels. She kneeled down in front of Granny. "Are you all right, Granny? I was so worried when I heard."

Granny reached out a hand and ran it over Madison's head. "I'm fine, great-granddaughter. No need for you to have rushed over here from—*there*. Where's that handsome beau of yours?"

"Right here, Granny," said Zack, as he kneeled next to Madison. "Are you okay?"

"I'm fine, young one, I'm fine. Thank you for coming to check on me, though. It's nice to know that as old as I am there are still people out there who care about me."

"You're not that old, Granny! Give it up!" said Kat affectionately.

"I'm just trying to get as much attention out of this as I can," said Granny crossly.

Kat laughed. "Okay, Granny, okay. You deserve it." Then she looked at Zack. "Oh, Zack! I'm sorry, but your horse is gone. I—"

"It's okay, Kat. Madison and I found him at the mouth of the cave waiting for me. We brought him back here, and he's fine."

"Well, thanks for the loan, Zack. And thank you for calling me."

"No problem," said Zack, "Mom." He smiled at her.

Kat smiled back and felt strangely gratified at that. It was the first time he had called her Mom. Not that Zack and Madison were married yet—but it felt good that he considered her like that. She sighed and said, "I better go back and get my med kit from the good doctor, and see how he's faring with those books that I brought him."

Everyone looked at her in surprise. They knew the implications of what the books meant. Doc now knew *when* they all came from.

CHAPTER EIGHTEEN

DOC STARED AT the backpack as he finished wiping down the examining table. Books? She had brought him books? What kind of books would she bring him? When he finished, he rushed over to the bag she had called a backpack. It had straps that had gone over Kat's shoulders. It was sealed with some sort of metal connector, and he couldn't get it to open. The metal fastener wouldn't give no matter how much he pulled and tugged. There was a small metal tab sticking out, and he tried pulling on that. It still wouldn't open. Through the outside of the bag, he could feel Kat's medical kit and five books underneath it. Five new books! He had to figure out how to get the bag open. Thinking that the metal tab was the key, he began to pull at it from different directions. Voila! It came open a small amount. He kept working at it, and realized that if you held it correctly and pulled at it from the correct angle, it came right open. Where would she get such a crazy fastener?

Doc pulled Kat's medical kit out of the bag. It was surprisingly heavy. He put it on the chair beside him. Then he reached in expectantly and pulled out the first book. The cover was bright and colorful. He hurriedly opened it and leafed through it. After doing the same with all five books, he picked them up and took them into the kitchen, setting them on the table.

Doc had never seen books such as these. He felt like Kat had given him a gold mine! The five books were on different subjects: medical diagnosis and treatment, medical physiology, internal medicine, history of doctors and medicine, and a book on a man named Louis Pasteur.

Flipping through the pages of the medical physiology book, he was delighted to find that some of the pages were transparent so you could see through them. The series of pictures started with a naked human being. You'd turn the page, and you could see the muscles. Turn another page, and you could see the circulatory system. Turn the page again, and you could see the bones. What an amazing book! He'd never seen anything like it.

After studying those few pages for several minutes, he set the book down and picked up the book about diagnosis and treatment. It had pictures of strange machines, and there were words in there that he didn't understand. That worried Doc. Had everything changed so much since he had been in school? Wouldn't his friend from Boston have told him about these new miraculous inventions? Surely the large hospital he worked at in Boston would have utilized such new discoveries for the welfare of their patients.

Doc had started going through the books with a smile a mile wide plastered on his face. Now that smile faded. He couldn't believe he had become so outdated and out of touch with the new medicine in so short a time. Then he picked up the book about the history of medicine. Doc thought that was an odd choice for a book for Kat to give him. Wondering what year the book stopped at, he turned to the back. The last entry was for 2012. What did it mean 2012? Was it a new way to signify the year? Had even that changed? Then he read the entry: the first womb transplant takes place. What did womb transplant mean? Confused, Doc turned toward the front of the book to look at the publishing date. It said it was published in 2013. There it was again—that strange date designation. Whatever could that possibly mean?

A thought entered Doc's head and a funny feeling ran through Doc's body making him shiver. He remembered the first time he had met Kat, when Josiah had gotten shot. She had asked Doc to wash his hands, and when he had objected, she had put her hands on her hips and said that she was from the future. Doc remembered that he had given her a smart-aleck answer that he was from the moon. He shivered again. Could Kat—and the rest of her family—really be from the future? Was it even possible? Did Josiah know? Is that where Zack moved to? Doc was shaking his head with his hands on top of the closed books when Kat walked into the examining room and called to him.

CHAPTER NINETEEN

"Doc? You in here?"

"In here," said Doc flatly.

"Oh, good, you found the books." Then she saw the look on his face. "Okay, so now you know. What of it?"

"I'm stunned, that's all. All these miraculous things. And what is a womb transplant?"

"You know what a womb is, right?"

"Madam, I'm a doctor. Of course I know what a womb is. It's the same as a uterus."

"And do you know what a transplant is?"

"Certainly. Sometimes you need to transplant flowers from one place to another."

"That's not exactly it. Transplanting, in reference to humans, means to remove an organ that no longer works, such as a heart, and replace it with one that does. The first heart transplant was in the 1960s—a mechanical heart—but it wasn't really successful. Later they used a human heart from someone else. It was a miracle surgery back then—now it's done all the time."

Doc slowly shook his head back and forth. "What amazing things have happened in a hundred years. So

70

this womb transplant thing happened in 2012, the book was published in 2013, what year is it in your world right now?"

"2014."

"I want to see these things. You know. In person. Is that possible? I've been sitting here thinking about it, and that must be where Zack has moved to—the future. Is that correct?"

"Yes, that's where Zack lives now."

"And Jenna, Ryan, Granny—they're all from the future, too?" Then a thought occurred to Doc. "Is Rachel from the future?"

"Yes, Rachel, too. And Sarah—you know, Matthew at the saloon? His new wife."

"I know Sarah. I loaned her my wagon to take Zack away—to the future—when he was sick. What did you do for Zack? How did you cure him? I was so happy that something worked. No matter what I did for the boy, his arm kept getting worse and worse."

"There's a new drug, discovered in the 1920s, called penicillin. It's like a miracle drug."

"When Zack returned to town, I couldn't believe the change in him. In a week, his arm was almost completely healed."

Kat nodded thoughtfully. "In answer to your previous question, Doc. Yes, you can come to the future and see some of these things in person. I'd be happy to show you."

Doc brightened. "This has been so overwhelming for me, Kat. I'm almost afraid to go. I'll find out how incompetent I am."

"You're not incompetent, Doc. You're a doctor from 1870. You didn't know about any of this. You didn't know about washing your hands. No one would expect you to know that."

"So washing hands is standard practice in the future?"

"Very much so. And now, very thin plastic gloves are worn, also. I have a lot to show you."

"Is there a library there? Can you take me there, too? I haven't been to a library since I left medical school and moved here."

Kat nodded. "There's a good one where Zack and Madison go to college. I think you'll enjoy it. When did you want to go?"

"Tomorrow?" asked Doc hopefully.

Kat laughed. "That's a little too soon. I have decided to move here temporarily for Jenna—no offense to you, Doc."

"None taken—especially after I know where you come from. How about Tuesday?"

"Monday, I need to reschedule all my appointments and call all my patients. I'm hoping to finish by Tuesday. Yes, Tuesday might work. Do you have a horse that you can ride over?"

"Um, something like that." Doc moved in his chair uncomfortably, but Kat didn't notice.

"You've been to Jenna's ranch, I know. So you know where the Red Bluff sign is? Can you meet me there? Say nine o'clock on Tuesday?"

"Sure! I'll be there!"

"There's a side trail just down from there—toward Jenna's ranch. I'll be coming out of there. Look for me."

"Okay!"

"I need to head home now. I didn't expect to be here today, and I need to go home and finish packing." Kat stood up and walked back to the examining room. She kneeled down, put her medical kit inside the backpack, and zipped it up.

Doc said from the doorway, "Kat, thank you. Thank you for everything."

Kat smiled up at him. "Thank you for taking such good care of Granny." She stood up. "Oh, Doc. Do you have any gold coins?"

Doc looked indignant. "Madam. You are charging me to go to the future?"

Kat laughed. "No, Doc. But I thought that if you wanted to buy something there—like more books—you might want to take some money."

Doc reached into his pocket and pulled out some coins. "Do they have to be gold?"

"I don't know that much about the money exchange. Zack is the expert on that. He was in town a few minutes ago. I bet he's still here. Anyway, I need to leave. I'll see you in a couple of days, Doc. Good-bye."

Doc looked at her warmly. "Good-bye, Kat." She walked out the door. He sighed and said to himself, "Good-bye, Kat. See ya soon."

After putting his precious, new books upstairs on his desk to keep them safe, he walked back downstairs. Checking to see that everything in his examining room was in order, he stepped out the front door and hurried up the street to find Zack.

CHAPTER TWENTY

KAT WOKE UP fifteen minutes before the alarm rang with a smile on her face, and she felt wonderful. She felt light and breezy and as if she was walking on air. Except she wasn't walking—she was still lying in bed. Still, walking on air was the best way for her to describe how she felt at that instant. Why did she feel this way? Going over the events of the past few days, she thought about canceling her practice for the next couple of months. No, that felt okay, but it wasn't the reason she felt this way. Moving temporarily to the old Red Bluff? No, that was just the pragmatic way to handle Jenna's pregnancy and her refusal to have her baby here. What could it be then— this feeling that made her all tingly and happy all over?

She thought back to Granny's injury, how well Doc did the stitches, and the look on his face when the books she had given him made him realize *when* she was from. Smiling at the thought of that, she realized that she was looking forward to seeing him again and looking forward to showing him around.

It was *Doc* that made her feel all light and tingly. Kat couldn't remember the last time she had looked forward to a man's company. Her smile faded. She *was* looking forward to his company, and that scared her. After what happened with Billy—his death—she was afraid to be vulnerable to a man again, afraid to let anyone in. Although she was so young when it happened, so very young, thought Kat, Billy's death—the loss of him—had made an indelible impression on her. It was a constant reminder not to give her heart away so easily when it could be torn away without warning.

It wasn't just Billy's death that had disturbed her so much. It was the suddenness of it. He was there one moment and gone the next. And she never had a chance to say good-bye—to tell him how much she loved him, and that she would love him forever. Kat sighed. She was sixteen years old when he had died and left her all alone in the world. Although she could have moved back home with her parents after his death, Kat didn't want to do that. There had been enough uproar in the family when she had gotten pregnant and insisted on marrying Billy. After his death, she had to do it on her own.

Even after Madison was born, Kat had taken Billy's death so hard that she felt alienated from her new baby. Where she could have poured all her heart into the baby of his creation, instead she held Madison at arm's length. Not literally, of course, she had read all the books. She had cuddled and coddled the infant as a good mother should. But she had held Madison at arm's length away from her emotionally, away from her heart. Kat didn't want to be hurt again. She couldn't take it.

The alarm rang, and Kat couldn't believe fifteen minutes had already passed. Swinging her legs over the side of the bed, she slipped her feet into her slippers and breathed deeply. Well, the gravity of all those thoughts had brought her back to earth, and she honestly felt better this way. Walking around with your head in the clouds just wasn't realistic. Doc was just an interesting acquaintance, and she would show him around and be done with it. They might have some interesting conversations while she stayed in Red Bluff—temporarily—but that was it. And after Jenna gave birth, Kat would move back here, where she belonged, and life would go on like it always had for her—enjoying her work, getting satisfaction from it, and going home alone. Always alone.

CHAPTER TWENTY-ONE

WHEN RACHEL OPENED the door on Monday morning, Doc raced over to her, hugged her, picked her up and turned her around, set her down, and kissed her on the forehead.

"Does this maybe mean that you're happy?" asked Rachel, still recovering from the unexpected whirl.

"Ecstatic is more like it! I couldn't be any happier if I tried. Come on in. Coffee is ready."

"I've never seen you like this, Doc. What's gotten into you, anyway?"

Doc poured her coffee and his own, and sat down opposite her looking into her eyes. "You, young lady," he started, "never told me where you were from!"

Rachel leaned back against her chair and looked like she was surveying Doc. "Um, sure I have. You know, the next town over."

Doc shook his head animatedly. "No. Let me rephrase. You never told me *when* you were from." When Rachel's eyes popped open wide, he laughed. "Yes, I know. Kat gave me some books yesterday, and when I noticed that they were published in 2013, it was obvious."

"Tell me everything!"

"The most important thing first, Rachel." He looked at her conspiratorially. "I'm going there tomorrow!"

Rachel set her coffee cup down and clapped her hands. "Oh, Doc! You will love it so much!" Then her smile faded. "Oh, no."

"What?"

"You'll love it so much that you won't want to return. And I'll miss you!" she said without looking at him.

"Oh, Rachel. No, I'll be back. I'm Red Bluff's only doctor! Of course I'll be back! Don't worry!" He had wanted to tell her of his budding feelings for Kat, but Rachel's reaction to his leaving shocked him. Being so much older than she was, he never considered her anything but a friend. Could she have different feelings for him? Oh, dear.

"Okay, then. Well, whatever you do, Doc, I'm really happy for you." Rachel smiled at him.

Hesitantly, he continued. "I have been devouring the books Kat gave me, and I have learned so much already! I'm so excited about seeing some of the things that I have read about. Like an x-ray machine! It sounds incredible that a machine can see through the body like that. I can't imagine!"

"Yeah, and there's also CAT scans and MRIs and I don't know what else. I don't know if she'll be able to show you those, though."

"Whatever she shows me and teaches me about medicine, I'll be grateful for." Doc sat back and sighed.

"I'm sorry I never told you before, Doc, but you know, it wasn't exactly something you'd tell someone over morning coffee!"

"I found out when I needed to find out, Rachel. Of

that, I am sure. There was never any reason for you to tell me. Now, it's important that I know, what with Jenna having her baby and all."

"I had heard that Kat was moving here temporarily to help Jenna."

"She is, but another pair of hands couldn't hurt. Especially another pair of washed hands!" Doc laughed and Rachel joined him.

Their conversation drifted to other things, and soon it was time for Rachel to leave and begin school. Doc enjoyed their morning coffee time together, and he frowned at thinking that he might have to stop that if she had feelings for him. He didn't want to lose her as a friend. But it would be unfair of him to continue if she thought there was something more between them. Perhaps he was wrong in that. He hoped so. Regardless, he wouldn't say anything to her until he was sure. Even then, he would have to think of a gentle way of saying that he wasn't interested in her. The last thing he wanted was to hurt Rachel's feelings.

His mind drifted to Kat and his growing feelings for her. Those feelings were probably out of line, but after so many years without a love interest in his life, he enjoyed the feelings whether she returned them or not. The last time he had been so smitten was when he was in college. She had been a visiting professor's daughter, and when the professor left at the end of the school year, she had gone with her father. It had broken Doc's heart, but he was so involved in school, that he deliberately set his mind to the business at hand, and eventually forgot about her.

Doc graduated and eventually moved out west. Then his mother got sick and began living with him, and thoughts of getting involved with a woman completely left his mind. With his regular doctoring duties to the people of Red Bluff and taking care of his mother, there had been no time for another woman in his life. Now, however, there was time—plenty of time in his life for someone like Kat. And if there wasn't, he would make time.

CHAPTER TWENTY-TWO

KAT WAS ANGRY. She was so angry that as she stepped into her office, she slammed the door behind her, making the glass rattle and making her worry that she broke the damn thing. So be it. She didn't care. She couldn't believe that she had opened herself up to having feelings for the doctor. What was she thinking? That was the trouble—she wasn't thinking. Her heart had taken the lead for that one second of vulnerability and look what had happened. The unthinkable. Her heart had made her think of the doctor as *a man*, not just a colleague.

Now what was she to do? Kat briefly considered canceling her whole plan to move to Red Bluff. She had to keep reminding herself that it was only temporary. Still, it meant she would be around the doctor. If it wasn't for Jenna, she would cancel immediately and not give it a second thought. But Jenna was her little sister, and if something did happen while she delivered—well, there was no choice. Kat had to be there.

And the doctor. What was she to do about him? He was handsome in a nineteenth-century kind of way. Who was she kidding? He was handsome any way you looked

81

at it. And that look on his face after seeing *when* those books were published, and his excitement when she said she'd show him the future. But most of all what drew her to him was how he stood up to her when she was screaming at him. He had stood up to her in a calm and reasonable manner. Few men could do that when Kat went off. Not many *people* could do that when Kat went off. Her father could. But he was gone now.

Kat sighed. How could she even look at the doctor with the way she felt about him? He'd know! And that would ruin everything. And she couldn't be mean to him —although that tack had worked before with men—but she had said she'd show him around, and she couldn't be mean about it. That wouldn't be right. She flung some papers around on her desk, and some flew onto the floor, which infuriated her.

By the time she needed to start calling all her patients to let them know she would be unreachable and to set them up with her colleagues, she was seething with anger. All the charts were on the desk in front of her. The top ones were the patients who had appointments with her that week. They had to be dealt with first and rescheduled either with one of the two nurse practition-ers or with the obstetrician. Trying to calm herself, she called the first number.

"Irene? Hi, it's Kat. It's about your appointment to-morrow morning. Yes, I need to reschedule—with some-one else. Something has come up, and I will be unavail-able for about two months." Kat went on to give her the choice of her three colleagues and explain that she would be happy to make an appointment for her. But the woman resisted. "No, Irene, that is not an option. I will not be in the office at all for the next two months. Yes, today is my last day in the office, but I have no openings. I'm booked solid. Yes, think about it and let me know. Today. Good-bye." Kat wondered what was so difficult to understand that she would be unavailable for two months.

She called the next number and the next and the next. With each call—at least the ones that resisted—she got angrier and angrier. Finally, she yelled at one patient, said good-bye and slammed down the phone. Then the door of her office opened with her first patient.

Somehow, Kat had managed to get through the rest of the day without offending too many people—fewer than a handful, anyway. And she had made all her calls except for five more in front of her. Taking a deep breath, she started calling, and managed to finish all of the rest within ten minutes. Now she would deliver the charts, separated into three neat piles, to her three colleagues, along with her notes on who wanted an appointment and when they wanted it. Almost done.

Even as busy as she was all day, she had still managed to think about the doctor more times than she would have liked. One time would have been more times than she would have liked. And now she was stuck with show-ing him around the following day. Hell's bells. What was she going to do now?

CHAPTER TWENTY-THREE

KAT WOKE UP, frowned, pulled a pillow over her face and shouted into it, "No! No! No!" Pulling the pillow tighter over her face, she continued shouting until her voice went hoarse. There was no way she could get out of it. She couldn't even call him to cancel. Resigned to spending an entire day with Doc, she forcibly dragged herself out of bed. Forty-five minutes later—fifteen minutes longer than it normally took her—she frowned, sighed deeply, and left her condo. Driving over to the ranch to saddle Paisley, she wondered what she'd say to him. How could she keep up her end of the conversation when she didn't even want to be in the same century as he was? She exhaled in a huff, parked her car, and walked into the barn to get Paisley ready.

Several minutes later, she and Paisley were on the trail heading, reluctantly, to the cave. Paisley wasn't reluctant, though. She was happy to be getting more exercise. Kat was doing everything she could to delay the inevitable, though once she was on Paisley's back, there wasn't much she could do. She wasn't going to confuse the mare by trying to slow her down—Paisley didn't move that fast, anyway.

Soon they were heading up the trail that led to the cave. Kat and Paisley moved around the last bush that hid the cave, and there, on a mule, was Doc. Her delight at seeing him surprised her, and she tried to stuff it down. But the growing smile spread across her face without her consent. "You said you had a horse!"

"Madam, when you asked if I had a horse, my exact answer to you was, 'something like that.' Crackle is definitely 'something like that.' And he is a good something, too." Doc patted the mule on the neck and smiled at Kat.

His smile melted her in ways she didn't realize she could still be melted. She cleared her throat which still felt scratchy from all her screaming into the pillow. "Doc, could you please not call me 'madam'?"

Doc nodded his head. "Yes, dear lady, and could you please call me David? I like the way you say it."

"The last time I called you David, I was screaming at the top of my lungs!" Kat snapped. Then she laughed. "Oh, all right! Let's go. How'd your mule get a name like Crackle, anyway?"

"The way I understand it, when he was still a foal, he caught a respiratory infection. When he breathed, his lungs made a crackling sound. So that's what they named him!"

As they started down the trail, Kat turned around to look at him. "Doc, I just realized that you met me on this side of the cave. How did you find it?"

"Zack. After he looked over all my coins yesterday and showed me the ones worth the most, I followed him and Madison to just past the cave. Zack said he didn't want to take me any farther. He said this was it, though—you know, the future."

Kat nodded her head. "Yes, this side of the cave is my time."

"Where are we going first?" asked Doc excitedly.

"Back to the ranch to get the car."

"What's a car?"

"You have a lot to learn, Doc, I mean David. Very, very few people in this world use horses for transportation—mostly only those in very remote areas. You know a stagecoach? A car is like a modern version of a stagecoach, only everybody has one. Even Zack has one! He has a truck—it's similar, but also used for, ah, work—hauling hay, stuff like that. Zack bought a truck, though, because he liked the way it looked."

"So you'll take me in a car to where we're going? What about the horses?"

"The horses will stay in a nice comfortable barn at Jenna's."

"Jenna's?" asked Doc, confused.

"Oh! Not Jenna and Josiah's ranch—the ranch where Madison and Zack live belongs to Jenna. It was my parents' place. I was raised in that house."

Doc smiled. "I'd like to see that, then."

That comment made Kat's stomach lurch. He wanted to get to know her. She squeezed her eyes tight shut and clenched her teeth. I can do this, I can do this, I can do this, thought Kat. "We have a lot to do today, David, maybe later." Kat wanted to put off anything suggesting any kind of personal intimacy as long as she could. Keep it business and maybe her heart would get the message. But even spending this short amount of time with David had already made her feel so good. And that feeling made her uncomfortable. It felt good— and that's what bothered her. It was addicting.

CHAPTER TWENTY-FOUR

THEY TURNED OFF the trail and Doc watched as Kat opened and closed two gates without getting off her horse. A couple of minutes later, they were in front of a big barn. They dismounted and led the horses into the barn. Kat showed him where to put Crackle, and explained how the automatic feeders and waterer worked. Doc was already totally amazed, and he had barely arrived.

When they walked out of the barn, Doc saw the large ranch house. "So Zack and Madison live in there?"

Kat nodded. "But they've already left for school."

"How do you know without going in?"

"Both of their cars are gone."

"If they're going to the same school, why don't they go in the same car?"

"They have different classes. Zack usually goes in earlier and comes home earlier. Madison stays later. Zack is trying to double up on classes so he can catch up. I warned him about doing that his first term, but he's surprised me and is at the top of *all* his classes. I'm very proud of him."

"Oh!" Doc stopped.

"Yes, that's a car, David. Are you ready to ride in it?"

Doc swallowed. "Yes, I guess if that's the only way to go."

"Don't worry, it's safe." Kat glanced at him again. "Oh, we're going to have to go somewhere else before we begin our day. It's your clothes. They will never do."

Doc looked down at his clothes. "And what's wrong with my clothes? They're clean and pressed."

Kat looked at him and shook her head. "David, no offense, but you look like you live in the 1800s."

"I do live in the 1800s!"

Kat shrugged. "You look very handsome in your long, black coat, but it's not worn here. I can't cart you all around town looking like that. I just can't. You look like you're ready for an outing with the Victorian Society."

"Well, what's wrong with the Victorian Society? Why can't I be with them?"

"It's like a club that Jenna, Sarah, and I belong to. They wear 1800s clothes for different occasions in town —like the Cowboy Poetry Festival. And that was last month. Regardless, David, we need to get you some new clothes. Come on, get in the car." She opened the door for him, walked around the car, and then got in next to him.

Doc didn't know whether to feel offended, angry, or pleased that she said he looked handsome in his black coat. Before he had a chance to decide which, Kat turned something, and Doc heard a big roar! He held on to his seat with both hands. "What was that?"

"That's the engine starting. Don't worry." She patted him on the leg. "Put on your seatbelt. Reach over your right shoulder and pull it down. Yes, like that. Put the

89

metallic end in right here until it clicks. Good. You ready?"

Doc held onto the seat again and nodded. "I guess so." Kat moved something in front of her, and the car started rolling slowly along, backward. "Doesn't this thing go forward?"

Kat moved something again and said, "Here we go."

The car began rolling down the street faster and faster. But surprisingly, Doc realized that in his youth, he'd ridden a horse faster than the car was going. It wasn't bad at all. He loosened his grip on the seat, and after a few more minutes put his hands in his lap. "This isn't half bad, Kat. I think I'm enjoying it!"

She smiled at him and then kept her eyes on the road ahead of her. He loved her smile. She was so pretty when she smiled—well, he had even thought she was pretty when she was screaming at him. But he liked her much better smiling.

A few minutes later, the car came to a smooth stop in front of a building. He read the sign in front aloud. "Humane Society Thrift Store. What's that?"

"That's where we're going to get you some new clothes. Cheap. But they'll do."

"Is my money still good in this future of yours?"

"It's still good, but I'll pay for it now and you can pay me back after we get your money changed over. Your money is worth a lot more than face value here. Didn't Zack tell you what your coins were probably worth?"

"Yes, but it sounded too outrageous to be true. I thought it was the exaggeration of the young."

"No, he wasn't exaggerating. That's how he bought that brand new truck of his. Let's go in."

Thirty minutes later they exited the store, Doc wearing black slacks and a white shirt, and toting a sack containing a pair of jeans and a checkered shirt that had snaps instead of buttons. Kat had insisted on the jeans, but he didn't see where he'd ever wear anything like that. Doc smiled because he felt like a new man. He missed wearing his long, black coat, but he was comfortable in these new clothes with all the fixings. Besides, when he put them on, Kat had looked at him, nodded, and smiled. And he really liked that.

He put the clothes he had been wearing carefully into the back seat, and then he put the seat belt on. Kat pulled away into traffic, and as they drove down the road Doc watched all the stores. This place was some pumpkins, and no wonder Zack was captivated with it. A young man could have a rip-snortin' good time here. If he was a young man with no attachments, thought Doc, he might consider moving here, too. But like he told Rachel, he was the only doctor at Red Bluff, and he had responsibilities. Besides, once the novelty had worn off, it was just another big city, and Doc preferred small town living.

Kat's voice interrupted his thoughts. "We're here."

Kat had parked in a place with lots of other cars all around, parked close together. So many cars! There were more cars in this one place than there were horses in all of Red Bluff—his Red Bluff, anyway. When he stepped out of the car, he saw a modest two-story building with many glass windows. Could this place really contain all the wonderful new medical inventions that he had read about in the medical history book? They started walking toward the front door. He would find out momentarily.

CHAPTER TWENTY-FIVE

As THEY WALKED toward the hospital doors, Kat stole a quick glance at David. Yes, he looked fine. No one could possibly know that he was from a time more than one hundred years in the past. The front door opened when they approached, but Doc hung back. Kat turned toward him with a puzzled expression on her face.

"What's wrong, David?"

"The door! It opened by itself! Do they all do that here? Is it magic?"

Kat stepped back through the door and pulled him by the arm. "Don't make it so obvious that you're not from here," she whispered. "Be amazed when we're in private, okay?"

Doc chuckled. "Sure Kat. Sorry. Didn't mean to make a spectacle of myself. Don't worry. I'll try not to embarrass you too much!" He laughed.

When they walked by the receptionist, Kat said hello. They walked down a long hallway. When they arrived at the end, they entered a laboratory. The woman at the front said, "Hello, Kat."

"Hi, Julie. This is my friend, David Mercer. Is it all

right if I take him in and show him around?"

"Sure, Kat. No problem."

As they walked farther into the recesses of the room, Kat whispered to David, "Shhh. Don't say anything in here. Just look and I'll explain later."

"Okay."

They walked to the open door of a cubicle where a lab technician was taking blood. Kat looked at David and saw his eyes get wide as the technician held the needle in place and changed vials. He watched as the blood spurted into the vials.

After a minute, they walked on. "What was she doing in there?" whispered Doc.

"She was taking blood."

"Why?"

"They can do lots of tests on blood nowadays to determine various aspects of your health."

"She wore gloves."

"That only started a decade or two ago—when they discovered that HIV could be spread through contact with bodily fluids."

"What's HIV?"

"That's a long story that will have to wait. Come on." Kat led him past the rest rooms with clean glass bottles on a small table in front of the door. "See those bottles? People pee in them, give them to the technician, and more tests are run."

David shook his head in disbelief. "So much has changed."

"Let's go this way." They strolled farther down the hallway, and Kat opened a door on the right. Walking up to the receptionist, Kat said, "Is anyone in there now? Can I show my friend?" After getting permission to go in the back, Kat and Doc stepped through an interior door, down a hallway, and through another door. "Look at this."

"What is it?"

"It's called a mammogram machine." Kat hesitated. "In our century," Kat whispered and then resumed talking in a normal voice, "many women get something called breast cancer. This machine detects it."

"How does it work?"

Kat laughed. "You're going to think this is really barbaric. The woman puts her breast in here, and it is squished between the two panels. Then they take a picture."

"What do you mean squished?"

"Here. Give me your hand." Doc held out his hand, Kat covered it with her two hands and pressed. "Except harder than I can press."

"Ouch."

Kat nodded. "Ouch, indeed. Come on." They exited the room and Doc followed Kat into a room off the main lab. She motioned for Doc to sit in a chair and took the blood pressure cuff from the wall. "Hold out your arm. Don't worry, this won't hurt." She picked up a stethoscope from the counter and held it up. "You know what this is, right?"

"Madam! I mean Kat! I am an educated doctor! I happen to own one of those," he said indignantly.

"Oh, okay. I couldn't remember when they were invented." Kat inflated the cuff, put the stethoscope to his arm and looked at her watch. "Perfect," she said, as she slipped the cuff off his arm. "Your blood pressure is 120 over 80. You're healthy!"

"I could have told you that! Now explain this to me."

"This is a sphygmomanometer or blood pressure cuff. It measures your systolic and diastolic blood pressures. They have found that blood pressure greatly affects your general health and especially the health of your heart."

"Okay, so systolic would be contraction—so contraction of the heart muscle. What is diastolic?"

Kat raised her eyebrows. "You know systolic?"

"I took Latin in college. What's diastolic?"

"When the heart rests between beats." Kat opened a drawer and took an instrument out. "Here, look at me." Kat held the instrument up to his eye."

"You're shining a light directly in my eye!"

"All the better to see you with! This is called an ophthalmoscope. Here check this one out." She reached back into the drawer, put the ophthalmoscope back, picked up another instrument, and held it up to Doc's ear. And this one, an otoscope, looks into your ear. It's remarkable what a little light will do." As she started to put the instrument back, Doc grabbed her arm.

"Can I look into your ear, please?"

"Sure." Kat handed him the instrument, knelt down, and turned her ear toward him.

"Wow! That is some pumpkins!"

"Some what?"

"Oh, sorry. I didn't realize speech was different, too. It's impressive is what I meant." He handed the instrument back to Kat.

"Come on, I have a lot more to show you. Do you want to take the elevator or the stairs? An elevator is a small room that automatically takes you from one floor to another. I think we should take the elevator."

Doc cleared his throat, uncomfortably. "It is not that I am afraid of such a thing, but I would prefer taking the stairs."

"Okay, over here." They climbed the stairs and walked down another hallway past open rooms with mothers and infants inside. Kat stopped in front of a glassed room filled with babies in bassinets. "Look."

"Oh, that's so sweet. What's that in the back?"

"Those are incubators for babies who were born too soon. Those two look like they're almost ready to go home. But sometimes babies are born way too early, and this keeps them alive until they're ready to go home with their mothers."

"What is that hose going into the incubator?"

"That's oxygen to make it easier for the baby to breathe."

Doc shook his head. "Amazing things here in your world, Kat. Amazing things."

"You ain't seen nuthin' yet! Come on, we're taking the elevator to the basement." She took his arm, told him to close his mouth—which was hanging open, and gently pushed him into the elevator.

CHAPTER TWENTY-SIX

DOC WAS GRATEFUL that they were the only ones in the elevator. Because when it started going down, it scared Doc so much that he grabbed onto Kat's arm. She laughed at him, and he stood up straight trying to look nonchalant. It was an airy feeling, like nothing was under his feet. He didn't like it.

When the doors opened automatically, Kat stepped out, and he followed. She turned to look at him. "That wasn't so bad, was it?"

"I could probably get used to it," he grumbled.

"You'll find this interesting." They walked into a room with two people sitting in comfortable chairs with their legs up. Each person had one arm stretched out with tubes leading into it. "Take a good look, then let's go."

When they walked out of the room, Doc said, "What is that?"

"That's kidney dialysis. Those people's kidneys are not working properly. So until they can have a kidney transplant, they come here to have their blood filtered."

Doc shook his head. "Amazing. Just amazing. What else?"

Kat laughed at him. He loved the sound of her laughter. He loved the way her face looked when she laughed. Something tight gripped in his stomach. Oh no, he was smitten with her. Plain and simple. He was smitten. The tight feeling relaxed, and he realized he didn't care.

"Let me see if I can find something that would interest you." They continued down the hallway, with Kat peering into some of the open rooms. "Ah, here we go, come in."

It was a small room with something odd in a frame on the wall, with an even odder picture on it. Kat touched something on the side of it, and a light came on illuminating the strange picture. "Do you know what that is?"

"It's a femur! A broken femur!"

"Exactly. This is an x-ray. If a bone is broken or suspected broken, the person has an x-ray so the doctor can see exactly where and how it is broken."

"It's like magic!"

"Practically. David, I'm getting hungry, have you had enough for today?"

"No, not really, but I'm hungry, too. I don't think I'll ever have enough of this, Kat! It's some pumpkins!"

Kat laughed again, and he enjoyed it so much. He studied her face as they walked, hoping she didn't notice. She had a beautiful face, with perfect green eyes and a cute nose, and the way her mouth turned up when she smiled completely undid him.

"Here we are. You ready for another ride?"

Doc looked around. "Can't we take the stairs?"

"Come on!" The elevator doors opened, and Kat pulled him inside.

Doc braced himself on the back wall, but when Kat pushed the button, he noticed how slender and beautiful even her fingers were. Then he got caught up admiring her again, and before he knew it, the doors opened. He stepped out and smiled. "That wasn't bad at all!"

They walked back to the car, and Doc got in and buckled his seat belt. "Are there any restaurants around here?"

"Plenty," said Kat, as she backed the car out of the parking place. She pulled out into the street, and a minute later was on a more major street. He could tell because there were more cars going in each direction. "There's one. There's another, and another." Kat was pointing out her window and across to his right. "There's the Thai restaurant that Jenna and Sarah are so fond of. But we're not going there. Are you a picky eater?"

"What do you mean?"

"Will you eat anything?"

"Anything within reason!"

"Good. We're going to a Greek restaurant that I really love. Here we are."

Kat parked the car, and they both got out. As they walked toward the door, Doc read the sign: Ambrosia Greek Restaurant. "Ambrosia. That sounds good."

"It's delicious. You'll love it here."

Kat put her hand on the door, and Doc motioned her away. "Allow me mad—I mean Kat. Allow me."

Kat nodded her head and smiled. "Thank you, kind sir."

They were seated at a corner table and given menus. Doc opened his and peered inside. He turned the menu and looked at the other side. "Is this in another language? Baba Ghanoush, saganaki, hummus, gyro, pita, shawarma—I don't know what any of that is!" He closed the menu. "I'll just have chicken."

Kat looked at him and smiled that beautiful smile of hers. She put her hand over his and patted it. "Let me order for you, okay, David? You'll like it."

"All right. As long as you don't poison me!"

The waitress came, and Kat ordered two chicken and gyro platters. She assured him that he would like it. He wasn't so sure, but he tried to trust her. Besides, he wasn't that particular about his food. When the waitress returned several minutes later with a huge plateful of food, he poked around with his fork, tasted the first bite and found it delicious.

"See? I told you that you'd like it!"

They ate in silence for a few minutes, and then Doc looked up at Kat. "When are you planning to move to Red Bluff?"

"I'm not moving there, David, I'm going there temporarily until after the baby is born."

"For how long, though?"

"I told my patients it would be about two months. That way, I should be able to stay on and help Jenna for a while after the baby is born."

Doc nodded and put another forkful of food into his mouth. He was thinking that he had two months to convince Kat to stay in Red Bluff permanently. With him.

CHAPTER TWENTY-SEVEN

THEY FINISHED EATING, and it was the most wonderful meal he had in a long time. At least part of it was that he was eating with Kat. And he liked that. When the bill came, he started to reach for it. Kat took it first.

"Kat," he said in a formal voice, "I insist. I do not allow women to pay for my meals."

She patted his hand. "David, you are welcome to pay for this meal if you want to. But not with your valuable coins. You still need to get your money changed over to twenty-first-century money. We don't have time today, so it will have to be another time. Then I will allow you to pay for my meal. How about that?"

"You don't leave me much of a choice, do you?"

"I didn't intend to."

Kat laughed, and when she did, he saw the sparkle in her eyes. He could get used to that sparkle. He wanted to get used to that sparkle.

Doc opened the door for her, and they walked out to the car. As they drove down the street, he looked around at all the buildings, all the cars, and all the people. Then he looked at the mountains behind the town. It was the same place but oh, so different. It wasn't anything like his home, and yet it was.

"That was a delicious meal, Kat. Thank you for taking me there." He leaned back in the seat making himself comfortable. "You know, I could get used to this!"

"Oh no you don't! Don't even think about moving here! It was hard enough getting Zack here—I can't do that again!"

Doc laughed. "I figured that would bother you. So when are you going to the old Red Bluff?"

"I'm almost packed. Probably tomorrow if I can get finished, and I think I will. I already called all my patients and had them temporarily transferred to colleagues. So I might as well go now."

Doc nodded his head thoughtfully. "Yeah," he agreed, "might as well."

A few minutes later, they were back at the ranch house where they had begun. "Madison and Zack are home." Kat pulled into the driveway and parked.

"How can you tell without going in?"

"See that little car and the truck? The car is Madison's, and the truck is Zack's. Let's go in. You can see the house. There are interesting things in there, too."

"Nothing could be as interesting as what I've already seen today at the hospital. Kat, I was wondering. Some of those instruments that you showed me—could I buy some of those and bring them back with me?"

"Well, not the big machines, obviously. They run on electricity—we haven't even talked about that."

"I knew it had to be something powerful to make those big machines run, but I was so enthralled by what they could do, I kept forgetting to ask! But, no, I didn't mean the big machines, those small instruments that you used to look in my ear and my eyes."

"Sure, there's a couple of medical supply stores in town where I have an account. I can order them for you. No problem. Just tell me what you want."

"The ears and eyes instruments for sure. And the blood pressure cuff. I could use that, too. Is your stethoscope the same as mine, or should I get an updated one?"

"It's probably the same, but a new one wouldn't hurt. I'll order all those for you."

"How soon will they get here?"

"Not today. Come on. Let's go in the house."

"How soon, then?" Doc asked, as they walked up to the door.

"They're pretty quick. Probably tomorrow." Kat knocked on the door to the house and then opened it. "Madison! Zack! We're here!"

CHAPTER TWENTY-EIGHT

KAT AND DOC stepped into the living room, and Doc looked around. "More machines," he said, pointing to the television and stereo.

"Yup. I'll let Zack explain these to you."

A second later, Zack appeared from the hallway, with a big grin on his face. "Hallo, Doc! Welcome to the twenty-first century! Hi, Kat!"

Madison followed Zack into the room. "Hi, Mom. Hi, Doc."

"Zack, would you mind showing Doc the new stuff in the house—and the bathroom?" Without waiting for an answer, Kat continued, "Madison, would you mind if I used the phone in your room? I need a little quiet to call my office."

As Madison answered, Zack had already moved with Doc in front of the television. Doc saw Kat disappear into the other room. After the television and stereo, Zack and Madison showed him the kitchen appliances. Although he found them interesting and remarkable, they weren't nearly as amazing as some of the machines at the hospital.

When they sat at the table to wait for Kat, after Doc asked them both how they were doing in school and asked Zack how he liked living in the twenty-first century, he leaned forward conspiratorially and said, "Would you guys mind if I stayed here for a couple of days? I need to exchange my coins for ones more appropriate—I owe Kat some money—and I would love it if you could take me to the college library."

"Sure you can stay here, Doc. You're welcome any time, of course," said Madison. "Does my mom know you're staying? You seem secretive about it."

Doc coughed out a laugh. "Well, Madison, you're very perceptive. No, Kat does not know. But I know she's busy getting ready to go back to the old Red Bluff, and I didn't want to burden her right now."

"So—you don't want her to know," said Madison.

Doc chuckled. "You are your mother's daughter, aren't you, Madison? The truth is that I didn't want her to know until I was sure that it would be all right with you two if I stayed here. I want to go with you to college—"

"You can't just go to college, Doc, I had to—" started Zack.

"No, no. I want to spend some time at the college library. I assume your college has one?"

"Yes, a very nice one. You could spend all day there."

"That's exactly what I want to do, Zack. And one of you can take me to exchange my coins?"

"That's Zack's specialty. I'll let him go with you. Doc, you're welcome to stay here as long as you want, and we're happy to give you a ride where you need to go. Think nothing of it." Madison stood up. "I better go check on Mom."

"No need to check on me, Madison. I'm right here. I

just called my office phone to see if anyone had left messages, and I had fourteen messages! And I asked them not to leave any! So I need to go to the office, take care of all the calls, and remove voicemail from the phone. I can't answer calls from the old Red Bluff, and I don't want people thinking I'm ignoring them. Doc, would you mind waiting a short while before I take you back?"

"Kat, I know the way. Go out the gates, go to the right, follow the trail until I get to the cutoff, and then turn up the trail toward the cave. Did any of you ever consider that the trail is getting a lot of use, and perhaps you should disguise it in some way to avoid people wandering into the cave accidentally? It could cause some problems if the wrong person wandered through."

"You're right, Doc. I should do that. I can start this weekend," said Zack.

"And I can work on the trail on my end. Kat, Zack and Madison have been so gracious as to invite me back here. They can take me to the college library, so I can spend some time there, and Zack is going to take me to exchange my coins."

"Doc, no, you can't do that. Who is going to take care of the people in Red Bluff? What happens if someone gets hurt?" asked Kat.

"I know a very talented nurse practitioner who just happens to be in town temporarily—if you would consider filling in for me." He looked at Kat and raised his eyebrows.

"No, Doc, I couldn't possibly fill in for you. I wouldn't know the first thing about medicine in the nineteenth century." Kat shook her head and kept on shaking.

Doc smiled a broad smile at her. "You'll do fine, Kat.

It's just like medicine here, only not as convenient. You'll be fine," he said encouragingly.

Kat exhaled loudly. "Well, I guess I could do that for a day or two. But I'm not happy about it."

Doc stood up, walked to Kat, put his hands on her shoulders, and looked into her eyes. "You'll do it for me, though? So I can spend more time here? And don't worry, I don't want to stay, but I need to see more before I return. Are you okay with that?"

Kat gave him a reluctant smile and nodded her head. "Yes, Doc, I will. And you're right. I'll appreciate the twenty-first century a lot more after practicing medicine in the nineteenth. Not that I need to appreciate it any more than I already do. I love it here and don't want to leave. If it wasn't for Jenna—"

Doc interrupted. "And you'll order those instruments for me?"

"Yes, I'll do it right now when I go back to the office. And I'll have them sent directly here."

"Thank you, Kat. And don't worry about me, I know the way home."

"Okay, David, I'll probably see you tomorrow at the old Red Bluff, then. Bye." She leaned toward him momentarily and then jerked back, and walked out of the room. "Bye, everybody!"

Doc sat back at the table with Madison and Zack. "There, Madison. Satisfied? It's not a secret anymore," he smiled at her.

Madison shook her head and laughed. Zack stood up and said, "Doc! Come on! Let me show you a computer. It's really awesome! You'll love it!"

"Thank you, Zack, but can we save it for when I come back? I've left Red Bluff alone without a doctor all day, and I really should be getting back."

"Oh! Doc! Kat wanted me to show you the bathroom. Come on, it will only take a minute." Zack stood up and beckoned Doc to follow.

"Zack, the bathroom, whatever it is, will have to wait until I return. I need to leave now."

"Sure, Doc. Are you sure you can find the trail by yourself? I can ride with you if you're not sure."

"The trail is obvious, Zack. That's why I suggested disguising it somehow."

"Okay, Doc. We'll see you—"

"Thursday, I believe." Doc stood up. "Thank you two for everything, and I'll see you in a couple of days! Bye."

As Doc walked through the living room, he found that Kat had put his other clothes on the couch for him. Why had she leaned toward him like that when she was saying good-bye? It was almost like she was going to kiss him! Was that it? Had she almost kissed him? Remarkable. Just remarkable. Doc smiled at the thought.

CHAPTER TWENTY-NINE

KAT FELT HORRIFIED. She didn't know what had gotten into her. She had almost kissed David! On the lips, no less! It had been so comfortable spending the day with him—almost like they were already together. But they weren't together, and they would never be together because he lived in the nineteenth century and she lived in the twenty-first. And although she was going to spend the next two months in the nineteenth century, she would be careful and stay away from him as much as she could. Besides, she didn't need a man in her life. She hadn't had one since Billy died, and she didn't need one now.

After parking her car, she hurried into her office. Although she normally walked to the office, she wanted to get this over with. Thinking she had finished calling everyone and then finding out that she had gotten so many return calls, upset her. Taking two months off from her practice was difficult enough, but having to deal with these last minute details annoyed her. When she walked in, she immediately sat down at her desk and called the medical supply company to order David's instruments. It wasn't until after he had asked her to buy them that she realized she had never showed him her temporal artery thermometer, so she ordered that for him, too.

She thought about his furrowed brow when he was so indignant about paying for her lunch. Some of the odd things he did—the nineteenth-century things—really endeared him to her. Kat felt herself falling for him, and she realized there was nothing she could do to stop it. Yes, there was! She could stay away from him and push those feelings down so far that they'd never come up again. Nodding her head defiantly she felt certain she could handle this. It wasn't that big of a deal, and she felt certain that she could maintain her distance. Kat hoped she could, anyway.

The medical company was confused about sending to the house because they always sent everything to her office, but she managed to get them to understand. The instruments would be delivered by Thursday. She had also ordered him some bandages and disinfectant. And that reminded her that she wanted to bring some extra when she rode back to the old Red Bluff. Then she wondered about ether—which she thought was the only anesthetic available in the nineteenth century. She'd have to check the internet when she got home.

When she finished her order and had everything she needed to take with her, she started making her phone calls. They were not easy calls to make. They were people who had received her first phone call and who didn't want to accept that she would be gone. Kat had some tall explaining to do, and she hated the extra work. She was so sorry that she hadn't thought to disable the voice-mail on her phone before. When she finished all the phone calls, she did that immediately. She exhaled slowly and leaned back in her chair. Finally, she was finished and free to go help Jenna.

Kat closed her eyes, put her hands behind her head, and relaxed. Thoughts of David instantly came to mind. And although she fought them, they fought back and remained. He was so chivalrous! Men in the twenty-first century rarely treated her with the respect that he did. Men in the twenty-first century had never—after Billy was killed, anyway—interested her. She didn't know where her crush on Nick had come from, but it certainly hadn't come from real feelings. But her feelings for David, they were real. That's what scared her about him.

Kat imagined his arms around her. And she imagined kissing him. She thought about what would have happened had she not stopped herself from kissing him while she was at Madison's. Of course, it wasn't appropriate to kiss a man in front of your own daughter like that, but it would have been interesting. And she wondered if David would have responded, or if he would have pulled away. In her heart, she felt that he would not have pulled away.

Leaning forward on her chair and sitting up straight, she thought that none of that mattered. It wasn't going to happen if she had anything to say about it. She couldn't risk it. Standing up and grabbing her medical bag with the new supplies packed into it, she glanced around her office for the last time for two months, stepped out, and locked the door.

CHAPTER THIRTY

THE TRAIL HOME—back to the old Red Bluff—was easy to follow. Like Doc had told Zack, someone should think about disguising the trail before the wrong sort of person stumbles into the cave. That could ruin everything. And now that he was one of the few who knew about the cave and where it led, he didn't want to give up that privilege.

Heaven knows, he would not want to live in the new Red Bluff, but he did enjoy its medical wonders, and he knew he could learn a lot more if he studied there awhile. That's why he wanted to go to the college library. If he spent a day or two there, who knows what miraculous kinds of knowledge he might learn. And anything he could learn in the twenty-first century that would help him be a better doctor in the nineteenth century, was good with him.

His mind drifted to thoughts of Kat and the kiss that she had almost given him. He thought that's what it was, anyway. There was always the chance that she stumbled toward him, but he had his hands on her shoulders at the time, and she wasn't moving. No, he thought he was right about that. She had almost kissed him. Why had

112

she stopped? Because they were standing in front of her daughter, Madison? Probably that's what it was. Perhaps the next time they were together, he would be the one to kiss her. Doc liked that idea. Maybe in the twenty-first century it was appropriate for the woman to take the lead, but he was a nineteenthcentury man, and in his world, men always took the lead.

Crackle the mule stopped when they stepped into the livery. He knew where his stall was. Doc dismounted and called to Ezra. Although Doc sometimes liked to saddle Crackle himself, he paid Ezra extra to have the stall by the door and to have Ezra get the mule and the wagon ready for him if he needed that quickly. Now, he wanted to get back to his house to prepare for his brief trip to the new Red Bluff.

"Here, Doc, I'll take him."

"Thanks, Ezra. I appreciate it. Bye." Doc walked briskly toward his house, a short block away.

He walked in the door not knowing what he might find. Usually, but not always, someone knew where he was going. But he had been gone most of the day and no one knew. There was no one in the waiting room and no notes anywhere around. He stepped into the kitchen. Red Bluff was a casual place. Sometimes, if someone got tired of waiting for him in the waiting room, Doc might find that person in his kitchen drinking a cup of coffee that he or she had just made. It was a little intrusive. But Doc liked that people felt comfortable enough in his house to make themselves at home there. If people felt relaxed, it was easier to treat them.

With all his reading, he realized how often people washed in the twenty-first century. They washed themselves, they washed their clothes, they washed their bedding—Doc figured they washed everything they could think of washing! They called it good hygiene. Occasionally, if someone was really sick, Doc would have them stay in his spare room—his mother's old room. And it was so occasional, that Doc never even considered changing the sheets. But if he wanted Kat to stay there to take over for him while he was gone, he would need the place cleaned up for her.

So excited about returning to the new Red Bluff and going to the library, Doc took the stairs two at a time. He walked into the spare room, pulled the sheets off the bed, and walked back downstairs. Taking them outside through the back door, he found a large tub, pumped plenty of water to get them good and wet, added some soap, and scrubbed them good and clean. Then he dumped the tub out, rinsed it well, and pumped more water back into it. Just to be sure he had gotten all the soap out, he rinsed the sheets two more times. Squeezing all the water he could out of them, he hoped they would dry by the next day. Draping them over a stretched out rope, he stepped back to look at his handiwork. They looked and smelled clean! Nothing was too good for Kat!

CHAPTER THIRTY-ONE

YES, SHE SHOULD. No, she shouldn't. Yes, she should. No, she shouldn't. Kat's mixed feelings about David were driving her crazy. She had feelings for him, but she didn't *want* to have feelings for him. So she denied those feelings, then she admitted those feelings but pushed them away. Men! They were always trouble, which is why she had stayed away from them for so long. She didn't need that kind of trouble. Exhaling, her lips formed a pout. But she wanted it. That's what confused her. Why was she reacting to him like this? What made that doctor so appealing to her? That's what she didn't understand. He wasn't so special. She shook her head. But he felt special.

Realizing that she wouldn't come to any profound understanding of her feelings at that moment, Kat wandered into her bedroom to finish packing. It was like this condo didn't belong to her anymore. It was an odd feeling, and she had no idea where it came from. If you're thinking of staying in the old Red Bluff, Kat, think again, she told herself. That is not going to happen. Now get packing, for your *temporary* visit.

One bag was already finished, and after packing a few more items, she finished the second bag—her backpack —with plenty of room in it for her medical kit. There. Now she could leave the following day. That way, if David was ready to return to the new Red Bluff, she could fill in for him. That didn't exactly thrill her, but when she thought about it, what else was she going to do while she waited for Jenna to have her baby? The old Red Bluff was not a hub of cultural activity. There was nothing to do there! Reaching into her nightstand, she pulled out three paperback books that had been on her to-read list and stuffed them into the backpack.

After she carried the bags to the door, she flopped down on her couch and looked around. Her condo was comfortable, efficient, utilitarian, and strictly twenty-first-century. In short, she loved it. Where would she be living for the next two months? At Jenna's house? No, when the deputy sheriff quit the following week, Josiah would have to start staying at the jail house again. Surely he wouldn't leave Jenna alone at the ranch house. So she would probably stay with him at the jail. And there was no room at the jail house for Kat, unless she wanted to stay in a cell! That would be a definite no. It looked like she'd be staying at the hotel, where Granny and her new husband, Edward, lived.

Kat had seen the rooms there before. It would be small, two single beds, a chamber pot in one corner, a small wood stove in the other, and a dry sink with a pitcher of water and a large bowl. Good-bye twenty-first century, good-bye all the conveniences of home. She still didn't understand the attraction that Jenna, Sarah, even Granny seemed to have for the place. It was one step above camping. And although Kat sometimes enjoyed camping, she couldn't see doing it for the rest of her life. Jenna and Sarah did have composting toilets, though, so they didn't have to use the outhouse. Granny, the dear, old, irascible soul, seemed perfectly content to use the chamber pot and the outhouse. Accepting a huge change like that at her age! She thought if Granny could do it, anyone could. Of course you had to want to. And Kat had no interest in remaining in the old Red Bluff much after Jenna's baby was born. She'd stay about a month after the birth to help out, but that was it. Finished. Done. Outa there.

And then her mind, of its own accord, drifted back to thoughts of David. She liked thinking of him as David, instead of Doc. It felt more intimate. Jeez, Kat, it *is* more intimate! What are you thinking? She shook her head trying to shake off thoughts of him. But they wouldn't leave. Every time she thought of something else, those thoughts would sneak back in. No matter what she did, she saw his face, heard his voice, enjoyed his smile. Maybe she could do what they used to suggest to dieting women: imagine worms crawling on the chocolate, so it would turn them off so much they wouldn't want to eat it. That wouldn't work. When she thought of him, it was only happy, pleasant, comfortable images of him. Probably the hardest part to get around was how comfortable she felt around him—as if she had known him her whole life. Which was ridiculous, because he lived more than one hundred years in her past. But he wasn't in her past now. He was in her present. And those pleasant thoughts of him had hold of her so tight that she didn't think they would ever let her go.

CHAPTER THIRTY-TWO

DOC WOKE UP and jumped out of bed, eager to start the day. Kat had said she wasn't sure which day she'd ride over, but he felt sure it would be soon. And he wanted everything ready for her when she arrived. As he scraped the straight-edge razor across his face, he looked in the mirror and wondered if Kat would like him in a beard. He had been meaning to grow one, but it kept slipping his mind. He'd ask Kat what she thought.

He hurried downstairs and into the kitchen to make coffee. Rachel would usually be there already, and he wondered where she was. Then he heard the front door open.

"Doc? Doc! It's me! I'm running late today, I can't make coffee. See you tomorrow! Bye!" The door closed behind her.

Doc hurried to the door to try to catch her. He wanted to let her know that he wouldn't be here tomorrow and that Kat would be here instead, but when he opened the door, Rachel was already disappearing into the schoolhouse across the street. Ah well, he thought, I'll walk over there later. And if he happened to forget, it didn't matter because Rachel and Kat already knew each other, so it wasn't anything to worry about.

After drinking his coffee and going over what he had to do before he left, he rinsed out the cup and left it on the counter. He'd probably want more coffee later. Walking into his examining room, he went through each cupboard and each drawer, making a mental note of what he had to show to Kat. He was sure that she would be fine without him, but she was used to more modern medical equipment, and his ancient instruments might confuse her. Doc wanted her to be comfortable in his house. Doc wanted her to be comfortable with him. That could wait until later. Right now, he had to get everything ready so he could ride Crackle into the future.

By late morning, Doc was wondering if he had been wrong about Kat arriving soon. It was almost time for dinner, so he decided to walk over to the hotel to eat. He'd also check on Granny. Although he had run into her several times already, she would never allow him to check her wound. She kept saying it was fine and to leave her alone. Today, he would not let her get away with that, he thought.

Before he left, he walked out the back door to see if the sheets were dry. They were. Gathering them up in his arms, he trudged back inside and up the stairs to the spare room. He struggled getting them on the bed and looking good, but finally managed. Kat would be pleased. At least he hoped she would. Doc laughed at himself. He wasn't even sure he could convince her to stay here, and he had already re-done the bed for her. Shaking his head, he left the spare room and walked back downstairs.

After checking the examining room one final time, he

still wasn't in any hurry so he moseyed over to the hotel for dinner. When he walked in, he saw Granny behind the counter. "Granny! Today I must look at your leg! No excuses!"

"Sorry, Doc. I'm busy right now."

Doc looked around and spread open his arms. "Granny, there's no one here right now!"

"Sorry, Doc."

Doc started walking defiantly up to her. "No, Granny, *I'm* sorry. I *will* look at your leg today. Now sit down."

"Oh, tarnation, Doc! Why do you have to be such a meddler?"

"I am not a meddler, dear Granny, I am a doctor. It's my job!"

Granny sat down at the chair behind the front desk and held out her leg. "Okay! Here you go, then. It's fine."

Doc looked at the leg and drew his head back. "You have new bandages. Where did you get new bandages?"

"My grandson, Ryan, brought some back for me—I mean, ordered some for me."

Doc smiled at Granny. "No, Granny, these bandages are not from this time. I know." He winked at her. "Who put them on for you? They did a good job."

"It was Edward, and of course he did a good job, I told him how to do it! You don't get to be my age without learning how to put on a simple bandage!"

"Are you slurring me again old woman? I ought to—" Edward held up his hand in a fist.

Doc quickly stood up. "You will not hit this woman —" he winked at Edward, "while she is in bandages!"

Edward laughed and gave Doc's shoulder a squeeze. "You know me too well, Doc. I'd sooner hit myself in the face than lay a hand on my beautiful bride." Then he walked over to Granny and kissed her on the head.

Granny stood up and pushed him away. "Oh, stop saying such sentimental things, old man, or you'll make me cry again."

"Well, I guess I'm no longer needed here. I think I'll go eat. Anything good today?"

"There's always something good! Go back there and get you some!"

Doc left Granny and Edward behind the front desk hugging, and he walked toward the back of the restaurant to his usual spot.

CHAPTER THIRTY-THREE

KAT WOKE UP, stretched, and admitted it to herself. She liked him. She really liked him. A lot. And there was no way around it, so she might as well accept it. If something was to happen with him, then let it happen. There was no way she could fight it anymore, because the mixed feelings were making her crazy. Her final decision came when she realized that fighting against those feelings was probably worse than going with them.

Although her bags were packed, and she was mostly ready to go, now that she had made that decision, she decided to take it easy, relax, have a nice breakfast, maybe lunch, and then ride over to the old Red Bluff. There was no hurry. She'd get there when she got there. After all, it wasn't like David was expecting her that day or anything. She had told him she wasn't sure that she'd make it on Wednesday. Kat knew that he was eager to return to the new Red Bluff, but she was quite sure that he wasn't sitting on the edge of his seat waiting for her to arrive.

After a leisurely breakfast and an even more leisurely lunch, Kat felt an unseen force pulling her toward the door. Kat's general attitude was to fight such things, but after a while, she couldn't do it anymore. "Okay, already!" she said aloud. "I'll go! I'll go!" She grabbed her bags and skipped outside, having to return a minute later because in her rush, she had forgotten to lock the door.

Kat made record time getting to the ranch house and brushing and saddling Paisley. Then she tied one bag onto the back of the saddle and slid the backpack over her shoulders. She climbed into the saddle, took a deep breath, and started on her journey knowing that life would be very different for the following two months.

When she got to the trail leading to the cave, she realized that David was right. That trail had been pounded down by so much activity, it was almost as wide as the main trail. That was dangerous—to the people of the old Red Bluff and to any innocent bystander who accidentally stumbled upon it. Next time Zack or Madison rode over to the old Red Bluff, she would talk to them about working on that trail to disguise it somehow.

She rode through the cave and out the other side, and soon came to the Red Bluff, Colorado, sign. Home sweet home. At least it would be her home for the next two months. That's as far ahead as she wanted to see right now. With a wide grin on her face, Kat rode into town and stopped her horse in front of the hotel.

She untied the bag in back of the saddle and walked inside. The first thing she saw was Granny behind the counter. "Hi, Granny! You have a room for me?"

"Hallo, granddaughter! You betcha!"

Kat walked behind the counter and gave Granny a quick hug. "How's your leg doing?" She pulled up Granny's skirt without asking.

123

"Hey, don't you get so familiar with me! That's my leg you're looking at!" Granny pulled away.

"Granny," said Kat in a placating manner, "may I look upon your lovely leg? Please?"

"Yes, you may," grumbled Granny. "But that doctor of yours already looked at it today, and he said it was fine."

"Where'd you get these bandages? And who wrapped them for you?" Kat knew that David didn't have any new bandages yet.

"Doc asked the same thing. Ryan brought them for me. And I showed Edward how to wrap them on my leg. I take care of myself, granddaughter, you know that."

"You're right, Granny. I do know that. You're fine. Can I have that room now? I want to get settled in, and then I need to go see David."

"Who the heck is David? There's no David around here." Granny handed her the key.

"Doc. David is Doc."

"David is it now? On a first name basis, hmmmm. I'll have to think about that one."

Kat grinned and shook her head. "See ya later, Granny. Bye." Kat took the key, picked up her second bag, and walked up the stairs to her room. It was exactly how she remembered the hotel rooms to be. She put her bags on the bed, sat down on the bed a minute for a breather, and walked back downstairs. No one was in the hotel lobby.

She walked out, grabbed Paisley's reins, and walked her over to the livery stable. "Hello!"

"Hallo, ma'am. Can I help you?" asked a tall, gangly man.

"I'm Kat, Ryan and Jenna's sister. I'm going to be

124

here for a couple of months. Can you take care of my horse for me?"

"Hallo, Kat! I'm Ezra! Nice to make your acquaintance! I suppose you're here to help Jenna with the new arrival then, huh?"

"That's it, Ezra. Thank you!" Kat waved to him and walked back down the street toward David's. She realized that she could hardly wait to see him. They could spend some time together tonight and maybe tomorrow morning before he left for the new Red Bluff. She smiled at the thought.

Kat walked into the waiting room, and called out, "Hello, David!"

"Kat!" Doc rushed out from the back. "I was starting to think you weren't going to show up today! So glad you did! Come on." He turned around and walked into his examining room.

"Okay." She loved the way he looked so excited to see her—she could get used to that.

"I wanted to show you the instruments that you might need and where they are. You know, before I leave."

"We have time, though. You're leaving tomorrow, right?"

"No, right now! I want to get there tonight so I can go to the college library with Zack or Madison when they leave for school in the morning. Here, see this drawer?"

Kat's smile faded and her shoulders sagged. For the following five minutes, he showed her the contents of every drawer and explained most of the instruments. Nodding her head, she heard most of it, but she wasn't in the mood. She wanted to have a conversation with him. Not this.

". . . and I have your room upstairs all fixed up for

you. Sheets washed and everything."

"Wait. What do you mean 'my room'? I'm staying at the hotel."

"No, Kat. You must stay here if you fill in for me. Sometimes people come in the middle of the night." He shrugged his shoulders like it was obvious.

She looked down and exhaled slowly. Then picked up her head and looked at him. "I don't want to, David. I don't want to stay here."

He put his hands gently on her shoulders. "But, Kat, you must. What would somebody do if no one was here to take care of them?"

When she felt his touch, she melted. She couldn't say no to him, when he asked like that. "Oh, all right. Show me the room."

She trudged upstairs behind him and told herself what an idiot she was to have agreed to this. The room he showed her was beautiful. It had the usual chamber pot, wood stove, and dry sink, but it had a beautiful chest of drawers, and a roll-top desk that was in mint condition. The room was so charming, she couldn't help but like it.

"Will this be okay?"

"Yes, David, it's fine. When are you leaving?" She asked it with a hope in her voice that he would stay at least a little while.

"Right now! Thanks and bye!"

He left her standing there at the head of the stairs dumbfounded. Next she knew he had grabbed a bag of his own that she hadn't noticed in the waiting room, and he had his hand on the front door. "David, wait! When are you coming back?" But he was already out the door and didn't hear her.

Kat was so flabbergasted at his abrupt departure—

and so disappointed—that she sat down on the top stair, and it was all she could do to keep from crying.

CHAPTER THIRTY-FOUR

Doc was so excited about going to the new Red Bluff and learning all he could from the college library, that he trotted Crackle all the way to the cave, and once they came out the other side, trotted all the way to the ranch house gate. When they arrived inside the barn, Doc untied his bag from the back of the saddle, unsaddled Crackle, and made sure his stall had food and water. Then Doc picked up his bag, walked briskly to the door, and knocked.

No answer. He knocked again. When he noticed a small button at the side of the door, he pressed it, not knowing what to expect. A loud ringing sounded within the house. Still no answer. Well, what do I do now, wondered Doc. Looking around, he saw that neither Madison's car nor Zack's truck were parked outside. It was late afternoon, so Doc figured—well, he hoped—that they would be home soon. So he sat down on the step to wait.

While he waited, he stretched his legs out and leaned against the door. Thoughts of Kat immediately came to mind. She had resisted staying at his house until he put his hands on her shoulders and looked into her eyes. It was like she had melted. If he hadn't been in such a hurry, he would have kissed her right then. He should have kissed her then. Well, he'd have another chance soon enough.

He wasn't planning on staying in the new Red Bluff that long. Just enough time to do some research and learn as much as he could that would be useful to him in the old Red Bluff. Those big machines in the hospital were wonderful, but there was no way they could be available to him back there. That reminded him. He never did find out about electricity, and that must have something to do with how those machines run. He'd have to ask Zack.

The sound of wheels coming down the road made Doc look up in time to see Zack's truck pull into the driveway. Zack smiled and waved. Doc stood up and walked out to meet Zack, who was getting out of the truck, carrying a big bag that was hanging off his shoulder. Kat had one of those, too. Doc would have to see about getting one.

"Hallo, Zack!"

"Hey, Doc, good to see you! Come on in." Zack opened the door, and Doc followed him into the house carrying his own bag.

Zack motioned for Doc to follow him down the hallway to the right. "This is your room, Doc. It's where I stayed when I first came here. It's comfortable. There's a television, and here's the remote control." Zack handed him the remote. "Remember how to use it?"

"I won't have any time for that this trip, Zack. I have plenty to read. But, thank you." Doc put his bag on the bed.

"Okay, now for the bathroom, Doc. Wait'll you see this." Zack showed the way into the bathroom, explained in detail how the toilet worked, flushed it a couple of times, and then turned on the shower so Doc could see it run. "You might want to try this before you go home, Doc. These twenty-first-century women like their men sweet and clean." Zack raised his eyebrows to Doc.

"Young man, are you insinuating—"

"Doc, chill. I've seen the way you look at Kat. I'll be right back." Zack shrugged his shoulders, then walked down the hallway to the room at the end. When he returned, he carried something small and metallic, and walked past Doc into the living room. "Let me show you this. It's totally cool." Zack sat on the couch. "Here, look at this."

Doc sat down beside Zack and looked at the object that he had opened. It looked like a small television, but the pictures weren't moving. "What is it? A small television?"

"It's a computer! It can tell you almost anything! What do you want to know?"

"I'd like to know what kinds of twenty-first-century medical equipment I could take back with me to the nineteenth century."

"Oh, I don't think that's something that it could tell us. How about, what does the inside of a human body look like." As Doc watched, Zack poked at the raised letters in front of him.

Doc watched as the picture on the front of the computer changed. Zack pressed something on it that made a clicking noise, and the pictures kept changing. Doc saw the skeletal system, the organs, and even something called chakras, which Doc had no idea about. Then Zack clicked again, and there were moving pictures showing more details. "That is amazing, Zack. What else can it do?"

"It can tell you almost anything you want to know—except the question about bringing stuff back to the nineteenth century. How about this?" Zack poked the raised letters again, and the picture changed to a list. Zack clicked and brought up a page about medical history. "How about this?"

Doc looked it over and nodded. "Very nice. But Kat gave me a book that mentioned all that."

Exasperated, Zack closed the computer, and sat back on the couch. "Doc, I guess you're not a computer kind of guy. Let me tell you about electricity."

Ten minutes later when Doc had heard way more than he wanted to about electricity, Madison's entrance into the house saved him from more of the same. Doc stood up. "Hallo, Madison! Thank you for welcoming me into your home!"

"Hi, Doc. No problem. You're welcome here anytime. It's obvious my mom likes you."

"Ah! Well—" Doc, flustered, didn't know what to say. But he'd think about that comment later.

"So what did you want to do tomorrow? Go to the college library? Can you find stuff to do there the whole day?"

"Yes, the college library. I will be busy there for as long as I'm there. I'm certain of that. They do have medical books there—?"

"Many medical books. The college offers pre-med classes, so they have plenty." Madison walked over to Zack and kissed him.

"Perfect. And Zack, can you take me to the coin dealer? Kat wouldn't let me spend any of my money."

"If you don't mind leaving the college library a couple of hours earlier tomorrow, we can go after my last class. Would that be all right?"

"That would be perfect, Zack, thank you."

CHAPTER THIRTY-FIVE

KAT HAD LEFT her medical bag in her backpack because she didn't realize that Doc was leaving. But she didn't feel like walking back to the hotel to get it. Maybe no one would come in this afternoon. She wasn't that comfortable about being in Doc's house and filling in for him, anyway. Although eventually she'd have to go back to the hotel to get her things for the night. And she had to eat. She hoped she could eat with Granny and Edward. While she was in the old Red Bluff, she'd like to spend more time with Granny.

Kat slowly descended the stairs and wandered around on the first floor. There was the waiting room, the examining room, and the kitchen. What was obviously absent was a bathroom. Finding the back door, she opened it and peered out. There it was. The outhouse. She hated outhouses. They stunk, and there was no place to wash your hands. If she decided to stay here, she'd make sure that Doc got a composting toilet like Jenna and Sarah had. Wait! What was she thinking? She's not going to stay here. No way. She would spend time with Doc while she was here, enjoy his company, and then she would go home to the new Red Bluff and live happily ever after—alone.

Walking back into the waiting room, she slumped down into an easy chair and a few minutes later had fallen asleep. When the front door opened, it startled her into wakefulness, and she sat up.

"You comin' to supper with your grandmother or not?" asked a voice that Kat recognized as Edward, Granny's husband.

Kat blinked her eyes, and he came into focus. "Oh, yeah. I guess so. Do I need to leave a note here or anything? I'm filling in for Doc."

"No need. Let's go. The old woman is holding supper for you."

Kat stood up, and Edward grabbed her arm and escorted her out. Edward pretended to be terse, but he was as kind and generous as he could be. He made outrageous comments like Granny, but he wasn't cantankerous like she was.

"So how long will you be staying with us, Kat?" He patted her arm affectionately as they walked.

"Probably a month after Jenna's baby is born—that is, if she wants the help. Jenna can be stubborn, you know."

"She takes after her grandmother, then. Granny's a stubborn old coot, but I love her anyway." Edward opened the door for Kat, and she stepped inside and turned toward the restaurant. "No, not that way, Kat. The family eats in there," he said, nodding his head toward the door by the front desk.

Kat tentatively looked inside the room. There was a sitting room in front of her, and to the left was a kitchen table set for five. Eliza and Samuel, who owned the hotel, were already seated. Edward, Granny's husband, was Eliza's father.

"Come on in!" Samuel stood up and pulled out the chair next to him. "No ceremony here. Just sit down!"

"Can I do anything to help?" Kat walked over to the chair and hesitated.

"Not tonight, you're company!" Eliza smiled warmly at her.

Kat didn't know these people well, but from what she'd heard from Jenna and Madison, there were no better people around than Eliza and Samuel, in either century.

Just then, Granny came out of the kitchen holding a steaming plate of fried chicken. Edward, who had gone in there after directing Kat where to go, followed Granny out with a plate of mashed potatoes in one hand and a plate of beets in the other.

"Everything looks delicious!" said Kat, as she sat down. It did look delicious, but she hadn't eaten anything fried in more than ten years. Oh well, she thought, at least it's organic! In the nineteenth century, everything was organic!

"Granddaughter, if you're going to eat with us, you really ought to be here when we eat dinner. I mean supper."

"Old woman, be nice to her. She was sleeping." Edward forked a chicken breast and put it on his plate.

"Sleeping? In the middle of the day?" Granny spooned herself some mashed potatoes.

"I sat down on a chair in the waiting room, and next thing I knew I was asleep! I didn't plan it that way, Granny. It just happened." Even now, as old as she was, Kat sometimes felt like fifteen again when she was around Granny.

"What did you need to see the doctor for, anyway, granddaughter? Are you giving advice or getting it?"

"Neither. David, I mean Doc, is, um, out of town, and I'm filling in for him."

"Oh! He went to that brand new future of yours, I guess," said Edward.

"I don't understand why anyone would want to go to a future like that, when life is so splendid right here and now," said Samuel.

Kat, shocked, put down her fork and looked around. She looked from Edward to Samuel. "You mean you've been there?"

"No, they haven't been there," said Granny. "They're both big chickens!"

"This," said Edward, pointing to the chicken, "is chicken. What we are, is uninterested."

"Agreed," said Samuel.

Kat looked at Eliza. "Jenna told me that you'd been there, Eliza. What did you think?"

Eliza shrugged. "I enjoyed the ice cream, but sometimes Jenna and Josiah or Sarah and Matthew bring some back for us. It wasn't anyplace that I could set store by."

"That means appreciate, granddaughter. You'd have to learn a whole new language if you decide to move here."

"Oh, no," Kat emphatically shook her head. "I'm not moving here, not even considering it. I'm just here until Jenna has her baby and maybe a while afterward, if she needs me."

"And what about—David—what does he have to say about that?" Granny raised her eyebrows, tilted her head, and looked at Kat.

Kat felt herself blush, and there was nothing she could do about it. "He has nothing to say about it. I'm filling in for him for a day or two. That's it."

"Old woman, let her have some privacy, or she might decide not to stay here at all," said Edward.

"Oh, shut pan, old man!" Granny looked at Kat. "That's nineteenth-century-talk for 'shut up.'" Then she and Edward looked at each other, bumped their foreheads gently together, and laughed.

Kat smiled. Since Granny had married Edward, she was the happiest she had been in years. It was good to see.

"They talk to each other rough-and-tumble like that, Kat, but they really love each other," said Eliza.

"That's obvious," said Kat.

"Maybe you could have that with—David—some day," said Granny, and then she cackled like an old witch on Halloween.

Kat didn't say anything, but instead tilted her head toward her plate and kept eating. Soon supper and small talk were over, and when Kat's tries at helping were refused, she excused herself and walked upstairs to get what she would need for the night.

As she rearranged her belongings, Kat realized how uncomfortable she was going to feel staying at David's house. What she also realized was how dreadful it felt being teased by Granny about something that Kat was already sensitive about: David.

Kat acknowledged to herself how bad it made her feel that David had left without spending any time with her. She knew why he had to go—he needed to get to Red Bluff before dark if he was going to get a ride with

Madison or Zack to the college library the following day —but still, since she hadn't expected that, it had upset her. And although a part of her said to forget the whole thing, the other part of her, the part that had melted when he had put his hands on her shoulders, said not to let that one thing bother her. He'd be back. And she'd be glad when he was. Until then, she'd be fine.

CHAPTER THIRTY-SIX

KAT SLEPT SURPRISINGLY well. The bed, made of feathers, felt good beneath her. And the sheets, though rough, smelled clean and fresh. David had done well cleaning up for her. He was endearing himself to her more and more. She was beginning to like the feeling. And she thought that maybe he even liked her.

No one had come for doctoring the previous afternoon, and no one had come during the night. With only one doctor in town, she expected some business while he was gone, but she was just as happy to be left alone. While she was extremely confident of her abilities in the twenty-first century, in the nineteenth she wasn't as sure of herself. With the limited supplies and instruments here, she didn't know if she could heal anyone.

As she stood in front of the mirror combing her hair, she heard the door downstairs open. Someone walked in. Well, this is it, she thought, my first customer. Let's see how well you'll do. Then she heard a voice, a familiar voice, though Kat couldn't quite place it.

"Doc? I'm here. I'll start the coffee."

Kat, curious, but slightly alarmed, walked downstairs,

through the house, and into the kitchen. There was Rachel, a friend of Jenna's from the twenty-first century. Kat had forgotten that Rachel had moved to the nineteenth century to take a teaching job.

"Hi, Rachel," said Kat slowly.

"Oh! Kat! Hi! I didn't realize you were here. Is Doc, um, upstairs?"

Kat smiled. "No, no. He's, you know, back there. In the future."

"Oh! That makes sense. He always gets the stove going before he shaves. It will take a little while longer since I just started the fire. Do you mind if I stay? Doc and I have coffee together every morning. It's become our little ritual."

Kat's heart sank, and her smile faded. Their little ritual? Was David involved with *Rachel*? It couldn't be. She was so much younger than he was. But here she was talking about their little ritual. It sounded more intimate than innocent to Kat. And she didn't like it at all. Rachel sat at the table opposite Kat, which made Kat wonder if she usually sat next to *him*.

"So what do you think of our little town, anyway?" Rachel looked at Kat and fiddled with her spoon.

"Rachel, I've been here before," Kat said with a little more force than necessary. But she wasn't happy with this new development. "It's not like I just stumbled into town."

"Yeah, I realize that. But it's different living here, day in and day out. I miss some of the conveniences, but all in all, I love my job and love the people here. I wouldn't leave for anything."

"Well, it may be a lovely place, but I belong in the future. This is not *my* kind of place. I'm here for Jenna's delivery and maybe a little longer to help her out. But then I'm done, and I'm going home. Where I belong."

"Each to their own, huh, Kat?" Rachel got up to see if the coffee on the stove was hot yet.

"I wouldn't even be here if it wasn't for Jenna's stubbornness. Nothing here interests me. At all." Kat exhaled forcefully and shifted on her chair uncomfortably.

"I'm so at home here, I can't believe it." Rachel poured the coffee into two cups. "Do you want sugar?"

"No, thanks. Just coffee is fine." Kat took a sip and frowned. "What kind of coffee is this?"

"Nineteenth-century coffee." Rachel laughed. "It takes some time to get used to it!"

Kat choked a couple of sips of coffee down. Although she wasn't sure if it was the coffee or the situation that bothered her. "Yeah, it's all right."

"So what will you be doing here while you're waiting for Jenna to give birth? Help Doc out?" Rachel sipped her coffee and seemed to enjoy it.

"That's not something that I've spent much time thinking about. Now that I'm here, I'll have to consider it. But I won't be helping Doc. He's perfectly capable on his own."

"Do you know when he's returning to town? I told him that he better not decide to move there like Zack. I'd miss him so much! But he was so excited when he told me he was going to the future! He went on and on about the x-ray machine! He looks so cute when he's excited," Rachel said thoughtfully.

Cute, huh? Kat had enough. Was Rachel trying to stake her claim to Doc? Kat stood up, picked up her cup, and put it on the counter. "Well, Rachel, nice seeing you. I need to get to work now. Bye." Kat walked out of the kitchen without ever glancing back at Rachel.

CHAPTER THIRTY-SEVEN

DOC WOKE UP early in unfamiliar surroundings, but quickly remembered where he was. The twenty-first century—the place that had machines that could filter your blood if your kidneys didn't work, the place where a bad heart could be replaced by a good heart, the place where Kat lived. What? Oh. How did that thought get in there? Then, Madison's comment from the previous day came back to him. "It's obvious that my mom likes you." Obvious to everyone but him. Well, except for when she leaned forward and almost kissed him. If Madison had been watching, surely she came to the same conclusion that he had. Kat had almost kissed him. Perhaps it *was* obvious then. Doc began calculating when he could return to the old Red Bluff to see Kat again.

Zack stuck his head in the door. "Doc! We're leaving in an hour. Will you be ready?"

Doc swung his legs over the edge of the bed. "Yes, I'll be ready."

"Great. Madison's cooking breakfast right now. Oatmeal, if you like that. There's plenty for you."

"That sounds fine, Zack."

"Oh, Doc. Listen, it would probably be better if you wore those jeans that you bought the other day. Did you happen to bring them with you?"

Doc laughed. "I had no idea when or why I would wear such things, but yes, I did bring them. Okay, I'll wear them."

After breakfast, Doc followed Zack out to his truck. They drove through town and up a short winding road to the college, which overlooked the city. Zack took him to the college library and dropped him off. Before he drove away, Zack called out, "Doc? I have an hour off after my first class. You want me to come back and show you some equipment that you might find interesting?"

"You mean they have more than just books?"

"Lots more. I'll see you in an hour."

Doc pulled open the big front door to the library. He walked through a second set of double doors and saw the spacious room before him. It surprised him so much that he stood still, just looking—until someone walked into him from behind forcing him to move forward. Row after row of tall shelves filled with books nearly reaching the ceiling. It was more than he could have hoped for.

Doc asked someone about the medical section and was surprised to find it was in a small room all by itself. A room full of just medical books! And he could browse through them at his leisure. Zack would be back in an hour, but he'd have to get back for his next class, so it shouldn't be too much of an interruption. And then Doc would have the rest of the morning and most of the afternoon to investigate all the books!

Doc began slowly walking up and down each of the

aisles perusing the books. He knew he wanted to look at a lot of books, but he had no idea where to start, so he thought he'd look until something caught his eye. Taking a book on physiology off the shelves, he sat down on a step stool that was for people who couldn't reach the top shelves. So engrossed in flipping through the pages, Doc didn't notice that someone was standing in front of him.

Zack grabbed Doc's shoulder and gently shook it. "Hey, Doc."

"Zack! I thought I had an hour before you arrived. I just got here."

"It's been an hour and a half, Doc. I got hung up after class. You ready?"

"I've been looking at the pictures in this book! They are remarkable!"

"Great! Is there a specific picture that you'd like to have?"

"Zack! I'm surprised at you! Are you suggesting that I should appropriate the pictures from this book?" Doc said gruffly.

Zack laughed. "No, Doc. I'm not saying that at all." Zack fished in his back pants pocket and pulled out a sheet of crumbled paper. After checking it on both sides, Zack handed it to Doc. "Here. Tear this up and mark the pictures that you want to keep. Then follow me."

Doc rapidly tore off pieces of the paper and stuck them into the book in a dozen locations. "Okay."

"*All* those? Goodness! Well, I should have known. You do like to be thorough, don't you Doc? Come on."

Doc followed Zack through the library to an area at the back. There were several machines lined up on tables against the wall.

"These are printers and copy machines. They are all

pretty much the same, except the ones on each end are for copying or printing in color. Do you have color pages in there?" Zack pointed toward the book in Doc's hand.

"Here? Oh, no. No color pages."

"All right, give me the book, and I'll show you how this works."

Five minutes later, all the pages were copied, and Doc was familiar with the machine and the process, in case he had more to copy.

"And if you want anything in color, be sure to use the machines on the end. Here's some money if you have more to print." Zack handed Doc five one dollar bills.

"I can't take your money, Zack." Doc tried to shove the money back into Zack's hands.

"Doc, you can pay me back after I take you to the coin dealer after school today. You can *borrow* the money, right?"

Doc straightened up and nodded his head solemnly. "Oh, yes. Of course. Borrow. No problem. Thank you."

"I was going to show you the microfiche machine, but I only have time to show you one more thing."

"What does the microfiche machine do?"

"You can read old magazines and newspapers from years and years ago. I'm not sure how far it goes back— but it might go all the way back to—" Zack looked around suspiciously and then whispered, "*your* time."

"Well, I probably don't need to know what was going on back then!" Doc smiled. "I'm livin' it!"

"Okay, come on. Follow me." Zack led Doc up to the second floor. "This is the computer area. Sit down." Zack sat down at one, and Doc sat next to him.

"I know I showed you my computer at home, but it

wasn't enough to catch your interest. So I spent some time thinking about it. Look at this." The screen came up and showed "Google." Zack moved his fingers on the raised letters in front of him, and "how does the brain work" appeared on the screen. Then Doc saw a tiny thing move on the screen to the upper corner, and something clicked when it was over "images." Suddenly, the screen was filled with many images of the brain. Zack clicked on one. "Look at this, Doc. I think you'd like it."

Doc saw a color drawing of the brain with arrows pointing to the various parts. One pointed to the amygdala, and it said *Responsible for anxiety, fear, and emotion.* "This is amazing, Zack! More! Show me more!"

Zack clicked around on various pictures, leaving Doc stunned. The pictures showed the brain in different ways with different descriptions, some of them more detailed than others. Then Zack stood up. "You can find the rest yourself, Doc. It might be hard to get used to, but you can do it.

"Before I go, I'll give you a brief lesson. This here is called the mouse. You move it this way. It corresponds to this on the screen, which is called a cursor. And this is how you click to make something bigger. See that? Choose the picture you want, then, using the mouse you move the cursor over it like this, and click like this. Got it? I have to run. I'm busy the rest of the day until we leave—about three o'clock. Is that enough time for you today?"

"Sure. It's a good start." Doc shuffled through the pages that Zack had copied for him, but moved into the seat Zack had vacated in front of the computer.

"When you get hungry, ask someone where the cafeteria is. It's not far from here. Oh, you'll need more money. Here." Zack handed Doc a ten dollar bill. "Now you owe me fifteen dollars, all right?"

"Yes, Zack, that's fine. Thank you. Good-bye." So distracted by the computer, Doc didn't even look at the bill. He just shoved it into his pocket.

"Bye, Doc." Zack walked out the door leaving Doc alone in the crowded library.

CHAPTER THIRTY-EIGHT

KAT WAS DISGUSTED. She didn't want to stay in the examining room, because Rachel would have to go through there to get out of the house. So she walked back upstairs. What she was going to do up there, she didn't know. But she had to get away from Rachel and that horrible conversation.

So Doc was involved with Rachel. Kat slowly shook her head and gritted her teeth. Kat felt like such a fool thinking that he liked her. He was just using her to get to the future and then using her again to watch his office while he was gone. And like an idiot, Kat had agreed.

She was furious with herself, falling for his charm and nineteenth-century chivalry. She had stayed away from men all these years just to be tricked into falling for that quack. Well, okay, that wasn't fair. David wasn't a quack. For a nineteenth-century doctor, he was probably as good as it got. But still, she was ashamed of herself for falling into the trap of being interested in a man. It was a trap, and a dangerous one at that. And she had fallen right in. Willingly.

The front door closed. Rachel had left and good

riddance to her. Kat breathed slowly and walked downstairs and then back into the kitchen. Should she have more of that atrocious coffee or see if there was anything to eat. She opened the free-standing wooden cabinets and found dishes, cups, glasses, and some pots and pans, but not one thing to eat. Not one egg, no oatmeal, no cereal, nothing. Didn't the man eat? Whether he did or not, Kat didn't care anymore. She'd walk up to the hotel and get something there.

Eliza, Samuel, Granny, and Edward had already finished eating when she arrived, so she walked into the restaurant and ordered some eggs and toast. Edward brought it to her. "Here you go, my dear."

Kat smiled at him. Her step-grandfather. "Thank you, Edward."

She ate it slowly, trying to savor every mouthful before returning to David's house. Halfway through breakfast, though, someone came running into the restaurant, breathless.

"Where's Doc? My dad hurt himself really bad." A young boy looked around helplessly.

Kat stood up and ran over to him. "Where is he?"

"At Doc's house. Where's Doc?"

"I'm Doc today. Let's go." Kat ran down the street, crossed the road, and walked quickly into the house, with the young boy following.

A man sat in the waiting room, his arm dripping blood and a shocked look on his face. "Where's Doc? I need him," said the man.

Kat stepped to the man, helped him up, and escorted him into the examining room. She helped him onto the table and said, "Sit there." Then she disappeared into the kitchen.

"Where's Doc?" the man asked again.

She returned to the room with a bowl of water, and a clean rag. "Doc is out of town. I'm Kat. I can take care of you." Kat always felt self-conscious going into her medical bag, but she did now, and pulled out a bottle of saline solution. She put some into the deep wound and moved the flesh around gently. Dunking the rag into the water, she began cleaning around the wound. "How did you manage to do this?"

The young boy stepped up when the man didn't answer right away. "He was whittling a toy for me, and the knife slipped. I'm sorry, it was my fault."

"Not your fault," the man said.

"What's your name?" asked Kat.

When the man didn't answer, Kat turned toward the boy. "Son, what's your father's name?"

"His name is Alfred. My mom calls him Alfie, and then he yells at her, so I wouldn't call him that."

"Okay, I won't. Alfred, I'm going to have to stitch you up. Are you okay with that?"

"Where's Doc?"

"I told you. He's out of town. I can do it for you." She turned around to her medical bag and removed some suture material and a needle.

"Will it hurt?"

"Yeah, sorry. Nothing to be done about that." Kat threaded the needle and had the boy hold his father's arm out straight. "Don't hold on to it tight. Just keep it steady for me, okay?"

The boy nodded, and Kat began. She carefully stitched up the cut, and then reached into her bag, spread some antibiotic cream on one finger, and nonchalantly, spread it on his wound. He wouldn't know the

151

difference, and it would help keep the infection down. Then she wrapped his arm with some clean bandages.

"I want to see you in a couple of days to make sure it's healing right. Can you come back then?"

"I'll see what I can do. Frederic, pay the woman."

"Okay, Dad. Be right back." Frederic quickly disappeared out the door, and a minute later returned with two large jars of canned peaches. "Thank you, ma'am, for fixing my dad. These are for you."

Kat, surprised, took the peaches and smiled. "Thank you very much. They look delicious!"

"Come on, Dad. You can rest. I'll drive home."

Drive home, wondered Kat. After Frederic helped his father out the front door, Kat followed. There was a wagon with two horses in front that she hadn't even noticed when she ran inside. Frederic helped his father up onto the seat, and then he took the reins while his father curled around his sore arm. Drive the horse and cart home. Of course.

Kat closed the door, sat down in the easy chair, and smiled. Her first patient, and it had been a success. Not bad. Not bad at all. She could do this—with only a little help from her twenty-first century med kit. As she sat there, she went over her morning conversation with Rachel. Maybe David was involved with Rachel, and maybe he wasn't. But Kat just realized something important. Rachel had referred to him as Doc. He had asked Kat to call him David. And David was more intimate than Doc. Maybe Kat had read everything wrong. Regardless, she hadn't even known him that long, and she'd already had more than enough drama. She was here in the nineteenth century to help her sister give birth. And that was it. She would take care of Jenna and then be on her way home.

CHAPTER THIRTY-NINE

Doc SAT IN front of the computer for another two hours, struggling at first with the mouse, and then getting used to it. And then the cursor was flying all over the screen, exactly where Doc wanted it. He checked out several different organs, and found the heart and the brain the most interesting. Although Doc was thoroughly enjoying using this computer-machine, his stomach was getting more and more insistent that it wanted to be fed.

Reluctantly, he left the library and asked someone outside how to get to the cafeteria. He walked in and was astonished. Standing in the back at first, he wanted to watch how everything worked before he stepped into line. Doc realized that he couldn't see what was under the glass, so he walked up to the front and saw more different kinds of food than he could imagine. At the end of the line, he saw the students reach into their pockets to pay. Okay, he thought, I can do this. So he walked to the back of the line.

The line was long but moved quickly. While he waited, he looked around at the students. Zack was right. Doc fit in much better wearing jeans than wearing

154

the slacks he had started with. Everyone in the large
room wore jeans—even most of the women. Doc had
seen Madison in jeans, but it was her house, so he didn't
think much of it—in the same way you might wear
pajamas in your own house. But he had heard some
students refer to some of the people as "sir." He as-
sumed that those men were teachers. And even *they* had
on jeans. A few of the women had on long skirts, and
one or two had on skirts so short that it embarrassed Doc
to even look in their direction. Weren't those women
afraid of their virtue, parading around half naked like
that? He would have to ask Zack about that. Perhaps
they were women of the night who frequented colleges
thinking the young boys would be easy prey to their
charms.

Doc was next in line. He copied the young man in
front of him by taking a tray and putting a napkin bun-
dle of silverware on the tray. Then he saw the food, and
his eyes lit up. Never in his life had he ever seen anything like this. Doc didn't think his tray could hold all
the dishes that he wanted to try, but by the end of the
line, most of it fit, with one small dish of jello sitting on
top of the meat loaf. When he arrived at the end of the
line, his food cost twelve dollars and seventy four cents,
so he dug out the money that Zack had given him and
handed it to the man, who immediately handed him
back two of the bills. Then Doc heard some coins jin-
gling, and saw them appear in a small device in front of
him. He didn't know if he should take them or not, so
he moved down the line until the boy behind him called
him back to get the coins. "Oh, thank you," said Doc,
embarrassed.

He found a place to sit at the end of a long table, and

began tasting everything that was on his tray. It was all delicious, and by the time he finished, his stomach was probably fuller than it had ever been before in his life. Relaxing back into the chair, he thought that it would be a good time for a nap.

Then he remembered where he was and what he was there for. It was easy to get caught up in this twenty-first-century life. No wonder Zack jumped at the chance to live in this place, thought Doc. And then there was Madison—a big reason that Zack wanted to stay here. Would Doc move to the twenty-first century to be with Kat? He wasn't sure of the answer to that, and now was no time to even be considering it. Besides, he had things to do.

Doc took the tray to the place he had seen the students clean and deposit theirs, and left his empty tray with the rest. Returning to the library, he resisted the draw of the computer-machines and walked back to the medical section. After he picked out several books that he wanted to study more thoroughly, he sat down in a comfortable chair to look through them. And that's where Zack found him two hours later, closing the cover on the last book.

"It's been a full day, Zack. I'm ready to go home."

"Not yet, Doc. We need to stop at the coin dealer and get your money changed. I want my money back!" Zack took the books from Doc, placed them on a cart at the end of the tall shelves, and smiled at Doc.

"You don't trust me with your money?" Doc asked soberly.

"Doc, I'm kidding, I'm kidding. I would have *given* you the money if you had let me. Let's go."

Doc followed Zack back out to the truck. A few minutes later, they wound their way down the road, and then Zack drove out into heavier traffic. Zack turned left and then right, and parked the car in front of a shop that had a sign in front: "Coins bought and sold here."

When they got out of the truck, Zack put two coins into something tall and metallic. Confused, Doc asked, "Is that what changes the coins then?"

"No, Doc. That's to pay for our parking. Let's go in here. But first, give me your coins. I'll take care of this. Don't say anything, even if it surprises you."

Doc shrugged his shoulders. "Fine. Here's my coins. Let's go."

CHAPTER FORTY

As Kat sat there thinking about Jenna, she realized that it would be a good idea to go see her and announce her arrival in town. She stood up, stretched, walked into the examining room, and tucked her med kit in the back of a wooden cabinet. Then as she stepped out the front door, she noticed Rachel across the street with the school children, and she got angry all over again. By the time she opened the door of the sheriff's office and saw a stranger sitting there, she was seething.

"Who are you?" Kat demanded.

"Rawlins."

"Where's Josiah and Jenna?"

The man shrugged. "They're probably enjoying their last few days at their ranch."

"Oh," said Kat. "Now I remember. You're the one who's leaving, so Jenna has to have her baby here instead of—"

"No disrespect intended, ma'am, but Jenna lives here, where else *would* she have her baby?"

"That's beside the point! Why do you have to leave now? Couldn't you have waited one more month until the baby was born?" Kat glared at him with her hands on her hips.

"No need to get all in a pucker, ma'am. I can't wait for a month because the new job starts next week." He held up his flat palm to Kat. "And before you say anything about that, the other part is that I'm tired of being treated like a no-account. I helped save Sarah, I haven't touched a drop of whiskey in several months, and everyone still calls me the town drunk. I can't live like that anymore. Oh! Do you know Sarah? She's the wife of Matthew, the saloon owner."

"Of course I know Sarah! And I wouldn't expect you to— But isn't Jenna giving birth more important than— Oh forget it!" Kat turned around, slipped through the door, and closed it hard behind her.

Now she'd have to ride all the way out to Jenna's ranch. It wasn't that far, but she didn't know if it was okay to leave the town without a medical professional. She walked into the hotel to find out.

"Hallo, Kat. The rest of your breakfast is still waiting, or should I throw it out?" Edward asked.

"Just dump it. But thank you for saving it for me. Can I ask you something, Edward?"

Edward made a deep bow in front of her. "Anything, milady."

Kat laughed. "I'd like to go see Jenna. Is it okay if I leave for a few hours, or do I need to stay right here in town?"

"Doc is always going off here and there. Just go and don't worry about it. Most things can wait, and if not, I'll send someone out for you."

"Thank you, Edward." Spontaneously and unexpectedly, Kat gave Edward a hug, and then stepped back out

159

the door. She didn't know why she did that, but it felt right. Edward made her laugh and treated Granny well. That was a good man in her book.

Walking into the livery, Kat called out, "Ezra!" When he came running out of the back, she said, "I just wanted to let you know that I'll be taking Paisley out for a few hours. I didn't want you to think that I was leaving without paying."

"Oh, I would never think that, ma'am. Would you like me to brush her down and saddle her for you?"

"No, thank you, Ezra. I can handle that myself."

"I'll bring you a brush and your saddle," Ezra said. Thirty seconds later, he brought two brushes and lifted her saddle and blanket onto the railing of Paisley's stall.

"Thank you!" She brushed the horse down until she looked sleek and fine. "You're still a pretty thing, Paisley." She rubbed her hands over the horse's coat, then hugged her neck. "I'm sorry I don't ride you as often as I should, ole girl. I've let other less important things get in the way. I'm sorry about that." She placed the saddle blanket, lifted the saddle onto the mare's back, tightened the cinch, and slipped the bridle on over Paisley's ears. Kat climbed into the saddle, stroked the horse's neck one more time, and said, "Let's go."

CHAPTER FORTY-ONE

WHEN ZACK HAD told him not to say anything even if he was surprised, Doc had no idea what Zack meant. But fifteen minutes later, when Doc walked out of the shop with nine hundred and eighty dollars in his pocket, he was surprised all right. What a peculiar time this twenty-first century was. He could trade in a handful of coins, amounting to less than five dollars, for more than nine hundred dollars. It didn't make sense. Doc patted the money in his pocket and smiled. But he liked it.

"I knew it would surprise you." Zack unlocked the car and stepped in.

Doc laughed and buckled his seat belt. "I'll say! I had no idea. No wonder Kat didn't want me to pay for anything with my money."

Zack nodded. "You can also buy old coins in there, that you can use in your time."

Doc shrugged and shook his head. "No need to do that. I have plenty of money for my needs." He patted his pocket. "But this money! I have plans for this money! First I have to pay you and Kat back for what I've borrowed. And Kat ordered me some instruments."

161

"Would you like to buy some books, Doc?" Zack slowed the truck in front of another store.

"I'd love to."

"Well, here we are then." Zack parked the truck, got out, and put money in the meter.

Doc, reading the sign in front of the book store, started bounding toward the door. Zack caught him by the sleeve to stop him. "Wait, Doc. Let me pay for these books, too, and you can pay me back when we get home."

Doc patted his pocket that was bulging with dollars. "But I have plenty."

"Please, Doc. Just let me pay."

"Okay," Doc said and opened the door.

It wasn't as big as the library, but it was still impressive. And he had money to buy any book in the place. He turned to Zack. "Do you know where the medical books are?"

"Sure, Doc. Follow me. The nonfiction is down here." Zack turned down an aisle, walked to the end, and turned right. "Let's see, it should be . . . yeah, right here."

"Thanks, Zack."

"I'll be over there, Doc. Let me know when you're ready." Zack walked away and disappeared behind another aisle.

There was one section of medical books, but when Doc turned around, he saw there were books on physiology opposite the medical books. Plenty to choose from. Twenty minutes later, Doc had picked out eight books. He was wavering on a ninth and tenth book, but some of the eight were hard covers, so the stack was getting heavy. And he had no idea how he was going to get them home. He should have driven his wagon over.

After finding Zack, who had a few books of his own, he followed him up to the front. When the clerk told Zack how much the books were, Zack reached into his pocket, and pulled a thin card out of his wallet. Then he slid it into a small machine, and the clerk gave him two bags filled with the books.

When they walked outside, Doc turned to Zack. "*What* was that? You didn't pay for the books with money!" Doc was astounded. "What new thing is that?" He pointed to the pocket that held Zack's wallet.

Zack laughed, unlocked the car, and got in. Doc stepped in and put on his seatbelt. "Come on, tell me."

Zack turned to Doc. "*That*, my friend, is called a credit card. Everyone here uses them—although money is still good. They charge your account, and then you pay the bill at the end of the month. That way you don't have to carry around a lot of cash."

"Amazing, simply amazing. Zack, how am I going to get these home?"

Zack laughed again. "Doc, you need a backpack! Come on. Let's get out of the truck. The thrift store is a few doors down."

They walked down the street toward the thrift store. When Doc stepped inside, he said, "Yes, I remember this place. Kat brought me here to buy my jeans a few days ago."

"Over here, Doc." Zack stopped in front of a shelf with several backpacks. "This is where I bought my first backpacks. Find one that you like."

Doc picked them all over, held them up, and analyzed which size and color would suit him best. "This one." He held up a medium-sized dark blue backpack. "I

163

think it will be perfect."

They walked to the counter, and Zack paid for the backpack. Then they got back into the truck and drove home.

"It's been a productive day. Thank you very much, Zack!"

"You're welcome, Doc. My pleasure."

"Why didn't you want me to pay for the books or the backpack myself—now that I have twenty-first-century money?"

"Because you probably would have pulled out the whole stack of bills to pay."

Doc nodded. "Yes, so?"

"It's not a good idea to show so much money. It doesn't happen so much in Red Bluff, but Madison warned me. There are thieves around who would love to have all that money. Just be careful, that's all."

This twenty-first century was a wondrous place, but not immune to dangers. Certainly there were thieves in the nineteenth century, but Doc had thought with all the new inventions and such, that dishonesty would have been eliminated. "I guess it's human nature, after all," Doc said, not even realizing he had spoken aloud.

CHAPTER FORTY-TWO

THE RIDE OUT to Jenna's ranch went quickly. After putting Paisley into a stall in the barn, Kat approached the front door. It opened before she could knock.

"I was wondering when you'd be out to see me." Jenna had her hands on her hips and a smile on her face.

Kat leaned forward and hugged Jenna. "Good to see you, Jenna."

"Come on in." Jenna stepped away from the door, giving Kat room to enter. "We had heard you were in town, so I wondered when you'd show up here."

Kat sat down and looked at Jenna. "I only arrived yesterday, and I've been filling in for Doc."

"Oh? Where's Doc then?"

Kat smiled. "Guess."

"You told him about the future!"

"I didn't exactly tell him," said Kat, relaxing back in the chair, "I gave him some current medical books. When he realized *when* they'd come from, he wanted to see everything for himself. I showed him around one day, and he insisted on returning. That's where he is now—staying with Madison and Zack."

Jenna smiled. "They'll take good care of him."

Kat nodded toward Jenna's belly and held out her hand. "May I?"

"Of course." Jenna pulled up her loose top to give Kat access.

"Everything feels normal. Baby has moved its head down."

"Already? Isn't this too soon?"

"You're in your ninth month, now, right? No, it's not too soon, but it also may not stay that way. Baby can flip this way and that right up until birth."

"Stop calling my son, 'it'," said Josiah, walking into the room and putting his hand on Jenna's shoulder.

"He's convinced it's a boy," said Jenna, resting her head on his hand. "I don't fight it."

"Unless you have an ultrasound, there is no way to be sure, Josiah. You know that, Jenna."

"A man knows, Kat. A man just knows." Josiah jutted out his chin and nodded.

"Whatever," said Kat. "We'll find out soon enough. So I understand you'll be moving into town soon?"

"Next week. Rawlins is leaving."

"Yes, I know. I spoke to him."

Jenna laughed. "You mean you tried to convince him to stay?"

Kat looked away. "You might say that. Actually, I may have been a little rude."

"That's nothing new!" Jenna laughed again.

"Yeah, well, I was angry about something else, and it just happened."

"Oh, what would that be?" asked Jenna.

Kat shrugged and looked away again. "Ah, nothing. Nothing important." Looking back at Jenna, Kat asked,

"Will you be seeing the doctor in the new Red Bluff again?"

"Our last appointment is Monday. I'll be telling him we're going out of town."

"Our last doctor's appointment and our last ice cream!" Josiah came around the couch and sat next to Jenna.

"Josiah, help me up, would you? I'll be right back, Kat. I have to pee all the time now!" Jenna disappeared into the bedroom, where the composting toilet was.

Josiah leaned forward and said quietly, "I'm glad you're here, Kat. I may be a nineteenth-century guy, but I'm not an idiot, and I know it would be safer for Jenna and the baby to be born *there*. She was thinking about it, but when Rawlins quit, she refused to even consider giving birth without me right there."

"I'm glad I'm here, too, Josiah."

"So when is Doc coming back?" Josiah heard Jenna returning and motioned behind him.

"I'm not sure. I didn't get the impression that he was going to stay very long. So I'm hoping he returns tomorrow."

Jenna walked into the room, and Josiah started to stand up. "No, Josiah. I can sit by myself!" She flopped onto the couch beside him.

"Where are you staying, Kat?" Jenna asked.

"I have a room at the hotel, but Doc insisted that I stay at his place while he was gone—in case someone came in the middle of the night looking for him. That hasn't happened yet, and I hope it doesn't!" Kat stood up. "Well, I should probably be getting back soon, in case anyone needs me. Don't get up. I can see myself out." Kat leaned over, hugged Jenna, pulled back, thought about it, and then hugged Josiah, too. "See you both later."

CHAPTER FORTY-THREE

KAT ALLOWED PAISLEY to set the pace on the way back, and as usual, when Paisley set a pace, it was slow. But Kat was in no hurry. Her mind drifted to thoughts of David, and she let it wander where it would. Taking everything into consideration, she didn't think he was involved with Rachel. There was always a chance she was wrong, but she didn't think she was. It didn't matter anyway, though. He may be attractive and interesting, but she didn't need a man in her life right now. Maybe in a year or two. Maybe never. It wasn't something she had spent any time thinking about, because she wasn't interested in anyone. And although Doc *interested* her, it wasn't going any further than that. She'd make sure of that. If he was even interested in her, which she had no idea one way or the other.

"What?" Kat said aloud. She realized that while she was daydreaming about the good doctor, Paisley had taken the side trail to the cave. "No, Paisley, we have to stay here for a while longer." Kat turned the horse around back toward town.

When she rode Paisley into the livery, Ezra was right

there. "Hallo, Kat. Can I brush her down and put her away for you?"

It didn't take long for Kat to decide. "Yes, thank you very much, Ezra. I appreciate it." She dismounted, handed him the reins, and walked toward Doc's house.

Walking in through the front door, she saw that no one was in the waiting room, and she was glad. Then she checked the examining room and the kitchen, just in case. Empty. It was getting later in the afternoon, and Kat didn't feel like eating with the family again tonight. She wasn't comfortable there, yet, and today she just wanted to eat and be done with it. So she walked over there, ordered something from the restaurant—she wasn't sure they knew the concept of to-go—but it was Granny and Edward, so they fixed her right up. Although Granny did give her some grief about not eating with everyone. So she promised that she would eat with them for Friday supper, and then she took her food home.

After eating, she read for a while, then went over all the instruments that Doc had showed her in the examining room. She wondered how David could get along with these antiquated things. He apparently hadn't had time to wash them all since he had gotten the twenty-first-century books, because more than half the instruments still had dried blood on them. Yuck.

Starting a new fire on the wood stove in the kitchen, Kat heated some water and began washing. When she finished they were all clean. She considered giving them all an alcohol rinse, but she'd wait for David to get back, because she wanted to show that to him. Although, after spending some time in the future reading medical textbooks, he would probably come back here and show her a thing or two.

The few hours before she went to sleep was spent either reading or wandering around David's place examining every inch of his space. She did not open any of his drawers, except the ones in the examining room and the kitchen—she didn't consider those private. But in her bedroom and in his, she just looked around, trying to get a sense of the man. Unfortunately, she liked the sense that she got. He was organized and efficient, and she liked that in a man. Men generally seemed like more trouble than they were worth, but David didn't seem like that at all. She exhaled slowly and pressed her mouth into a grim smile. Kat didn't like the way she was feeling about David, but she didn't know what to do about it. Ignore it is what she finally decided. Definitely ignore it.

CHAPTER FORTY-FOUR

FRIDAY MORNING, KAT blinked open her eyes, and her first unbidden thought was that David would be home today. She pushed down the part of her that was looking forward to seeing him again, and let surface the part that just wanted to let him go back to the doctoring in this town. It had been an interesting distraction, but she was ready to let it go. Although she had a twenty-first-century education—probably more schooling than David had —she was smart enough to realize there were injuries and illnesses that could happen here that she would have no idea how to handle. If the same injury happened in the twenty-first century, yes, of course she could fix it, or find someone who could. But here? With everything limited and half of what she knew not even invented yet? No, she wanted to give him back his job before something happened that she couldn't handle.

Oh! She jumped out of bed and ran downstairs in her nightie. Throwing some kindling in the wood stove, lighting it, and poking it around, she finally got a fire going. Then she put on a larger piece of wood and ran back upstairs to get dressed. Kat didn't want Rachel to think that she wasn't doing her job—as if lighting the wood stove was part of her job—Kat smiled. Whatever. Maybe Rachel would leave sooner if the fire was already hot when she arrived here. Rachel may not be involved with David, but Kat didn't want to hear any more intimate stories of the two of them or what David had shared with her. No, Kat wasn't jealous! She just didn't want to hear about it. That's all. Was that so wrong?

Kat finished dressing, washed her face in the bowl in her room, and was starting downstairs when she heard Rachel come in the door.

"Doc? Kat? Whoever is here, here I am!"

"Na na na na na na na!" sassed Kat quietly, moving her head from side to side.

"I'll start the coffee," said Rachel from the other room.

Damn, thought Kat. If I had thought to start the coffee, I could have gotten her out of here sooner! I'll remember tomorrow. Oh, wait. David will be back by then, and *he'll* be having coffee with her. That gave her a sick feeling in her stomach.

"Hello, Rachel," Kat said with a slight smile, when she walked into the kitchen and sat down.

"Thanks for starting the fire, Kat! It makes it easier for me that way." Rachel had gotten two cups out of the cupboard, set them on the table, and sat down opposite Kat.

"Doc not back yet, huh?"

Kat shook her head and shrugged. "Probably today some time."

"How do you like our little town?"

Our town, wondered Kat, and the smile slid off her face. "Didn't you ask me that yesterday?"

Rachel laughed easily. She was a good natured sort, and Kat had never minded her, but if she was infringing on *my* territory, thought Kat—

"Well, yeah, but you've had another whole day to decide! Do you still like it here?"

"Nice place to visit, but I wouldn't want to live here."

"Oh, Kat!" Rachel poured coffee in both cups. "You've always been such a spoil sport."

Kat sat up straighter, tilted her head, and looked at Rachel. "How can you say that?"

"Oh, Kat. Because it's true. You know it is."

"No, Rachel, I don't know that it is. Give me an example."

"When your folks were away to a horse show, and you were watching Jenna, and I'd be over to play, you wouldn't let us ride horses after three o'clock because you were afraid we wouldn't put the tack away; you wouldn't let us play video games in the living room because it annoyed you; you—"

"Okay, okay, point taken. But remember, you were only seven or eight years old then. You needed some boundaries."

Rachel shrugged. "Your parents never set boundaries like that."

"Well, maybe they should have!" Kat gulped down the last of her coffee. "Well, gotta run. See you later, Rachel." Kat stomped out of the room and up the stairs, but not fast enough to miss Rachel chuckling in the kitchen.

Kat walked back downstairs when she heard Rachel close the front door. She thought that she wouldn't even come downstairs the following morning until Rachel had left. No, wait! David would be back by then, and Kat wouldn't even be here to deal with Rachel. Oh, damn! That would mean that David and Rachel would have coffee together. Kat shook her head and tried to ignore the sense of growing dread in her stomach.

Not wanting to eat breakfast at the hotel with the family, Kat decided that she'd stay right there and eat some of those canned peaches. They were delicious and filling enough. She'd get by, anyway. When she put the lid onto the container of peaches, she looked around for the refrigerator. It took her a minute to realize there wasn't any. How did people live like this? Kat could hardly wait to return to her own time. It was too much trouble living here.

CHAPTER FORTY-FIVE

Doc and Kat were side by side, and Jenna lay on the bed in front of them. Doc reached down to catch the baby when it arrived, but he looked straight forward over Jenna's head. "David! What are you doing?" screamed Kat. "Look at what you are doing!" Before he could answer, Doc heard another sound.

"Doc! Doc! Breakfast in fifteen minutes."

Groggily, Doc shook his head from the strange dream and replied, "Fine, Zack, fine. I'll be there."

He stood up, got dressed, and walked down the hall to the bathroom. He liked that bathroom. It was convenient, and he didn't have to go outside. Doc wished that he could install something like that in his house. After flushing the toilet and washing his hands, he walked into the kitchen.

"We're having oatmeal again. Hope you don't mind, Doc." Madison put the bowl of oatmeal on the table in front of him. "Here's some honey."

Doc dribbled some honey onto the oatmeal and stirred it. "Don't be sorry, Madison, I love this stuff."

Madison picked up the container and showed it to

Doc. "It's called steel cut oats. My mom loves it, too. I generally don't like the stuff she eats—it's a little too healthy for me—but this is wonderful."

"Your mom likes it. Could I possibly buy some to bring back with me?"

Madison reached into the cupboard and pulled out a fresh container. "I just bought this one, but the old one isn't finished yet. You can have the new one, and I'll pick more up next time I go marketing." She put the container of oats on the table by Doc.

"I'll pay you for them." Doc said, as he picked up the container to look at it.

"No, you don't have to," said Madison.

"Yes, yes, I must. And I have the money right here." Doc reached into his pocket, pulled out his hand, and nine hundred dollars tumbled to the floor."

Zack walked into the room just then. "And *that*, Doc, is why I didn't want you to pay for the books yourself. That much money takes some time getting used to! Before we take off, leave most of the money at home and only bring forty or fifty dollars with you. Even that is probably too much."

Doc knelt down to gather the money together. It hadn't fallen in one pile, but had floated through the air and spread itself all around. "I can pay my own way. I insist on paying for the oatmeal. You've been very good to me letting me stay here and driving me everywhere; it's the least I can do." He stood up, stuffed the bills back in his pocket, and sat down to finish his oatmeal.

"Doc, didn't you hear about how much money Zack made with the coins that he brought back from the nineteenth century? We are *loaded*! We don't need your money! It's our pleasure having you here!" said Madison.

"Well, I don't know. I'll think about it. I'm used to paying my own way."

"Get over it, Doc. Get over it. I have an early class today. Will you be ready in ten minutes? If not, you can drive in with Madison in an hour," said Zack.

Doc spooned the last of the oatmeal into his mouth, stood up, and turned on the faucet. As he rinsed the bowl, he said, "I'll be ready, Zack. I'd like to get started early today."

When he returned to his room, he took his straight-blade razor, and walked into the bathroom. Forgetting to close the door, he stood at the sink, shaving.

"Hey, Doc."

"Yes, Madison?" Doc turned around to look at her, while still scraping the blade across his face.

"I can't believe you're using a straight-edge razor."

"What else is there?" He turned back toward the mirror.

"Something safer! See ya later!" Madison walked off, but Doc heard her say, "Zack, get Doc a decent razor to take home with him!"

Doc had no idea what she was talking about, but he finished shaving and walked out to the living room to wait for Zack. A minute later Zack appeared from the hallway.

"Did you leave your money in the drawer, Doc?"

"No. Do you really think I need to?"

"Definitely! Come on, I'll help you."

Zack walked with him into the bedroom, and when Doc pulled the money out of his pocket, it again fell all over the floor. Zack laughed. "See, this much money is hard to handle. Let's put most of it in the drawer."

When that was taken care of, Doc and Zack walked out of the house, got into the truck, and drove up to the college. When Zack dropped him off at the library, Zack told him that he'd be back to pick him up at 2:30.

Doc walked into the library and directly to the medical books. The previous day, the library had been a brand new wonderland. Today, he already knew where everything was, knew how most of the machines worked, and felt like he had lived here forever. He picked out a few books, and brought them over to the sitting area. Fifteen minutes later he was engrossed in the medical textbook he was reading. And thirty minutes later, his mind had wandered to how beautiful Kat was.

Where did thoughts of Kat come from? He was supposed to be studying. Trying to push her image from his mind, he returned to reading the book. There she was again, hands on her hips yelling at him for something. She looked so pretty when she was angry. And the way she had felt when he put his hands on her shoulders— and when she had almost kissed him. Doc closed the book. It was no use. Kat was on his mind, and she wasn't about to leave.

The morning's dream made its way back into his mind, and he found it strange. Why would she tell him to look at what he was doing? It just wasn't done that way. Surely, giving birth couldn't have changed that much in a century. He dismissed it as another strange dream scenario that didn't make much sense. But he couldn't get Kat off his mind.

Doc put all the books back on the cart at the end of the aisle. He decided that maybe he needed a break. Walking out of the library, he looked around and strolled down a path opposite from the cafeteria. Wandering all over campus couldn't flush Kat from his mind. He'd see a tree and picture her there. A car would pull out in front of him, and he'd move his arm to protect her from the car. When he managed to return to what he was doing, he marveled at how big the campus was, how spread out, how modern. He even walked inside some of the buildings and glanced in at the classrooms where doors had been left open. Well, classrooms hadn't changed much, but there were more people in them in this century. As he walked by one classroom, he thought he saw Kat inside, and he stumbled and had to look in again. It wasn't her, of course, and he made his way back outside.

When he had finished walking around and had been unsuccessful in getting Kat off his mind, he found he was hungry, so he entered the cafeteria. The main dishes were different from the day before, and he filled his tray again with almost everything he saw, careful to get the items that he had previously missed. Feeling stuffed when he finished, he decided he better walk it off before returning to the library. An hour walk helped his stuffed feeling, but did nothing to get Kat out of his head. And it was almost time for Zack to pick him up. Doc headed toward the library.

CHAPTER FORTY-SIX

JUST BEFORE NOON, an older woman came in—Granny's age—looking for Doc. She had a basket in her hand that she placed on a chair.

"My name is Kat. I'm filling in for Doc today." Kat hoped that he would return home early enough that she could be relieved of this duty.

"My name is Mary. Where is he?"

"I don't know exactly, but he asked me to fill in for him before he left." The woman had a runny nose. A cold. "What can I help you with, Mary?"

"I've got catarrh." She pointed to her nose.

"Come in to the examining room."

The woman followed her in. Kat had her sit on the examining table, and then she put her hand on the woman's forehead. Her temperature felt normal, but best to be sure. She quickly pulled her temporal artery thermometer out of her med kit, and just as quickly wiped it across the woman's forehead. Glancing at it before she stuck it back in the kit, she saw that the woman's temperature was normal.

Kat pulled a tongue depressor out of one of David's

drawers. "Open up and say, 'ahhh.'"

"What?"

Kat opened her mouth, stuck out her tongue, and said, "Ahhhh." Apparently the whole ahhh thing wasn't used in the nineteenth century, thought Kat.

"Oh, all right."

The woman opened her mouth, and Kat saw that her throat was mildly inflamed. "Mary, you have a cold."

"No! It's catarrh."

"It's a cold, and you'll be fine in a week or so."

"No, it's catarrh, and I want medicine for it. Doc always gives me medicine for catarrh."

"What kind of medicine does Doc give you?"

"Catarrh drops."

Catarrh drops, thought Kat. What kind of snake oil medicine was catarrh drops? She began going through the cupboards. She remembered there was one shelf with medicines on them. Yes, right here. There it was. Catarrh drops. Kat picked up the bottle and showed it to the woman. "This?"

"Yes, that's it."

"Um, how does Doc give it to you?"

The woman squinted and frowned. "You don't even know how to give catarrh drops, and you're filling in for Doc? Shameful! Simply shameful."

"Perhaps it is, but I can't give them to you unless you tell me how."

The woman put both hands on her hips. "Doc drops some into my mouth, and the catarrh is cleared up in no time. It always works." Mary opened her mouth, and Kat dribbled two drops onto her outstretched tongue.

"Thank you. Before Doc leaves you here alone again, he should teach you a thing or two." Mary got off the chair and walked into the waiting room. She pointed to the basket on the chair. "There's your payment for the catarrh drops, though I should take one back for having to tell you how to give them to me." Then, without another word, she stepped out the door.

Kat looked in the basket. Four eggs, safely packed with straw separating them. Kat laughed. "Well, if I practiced medicine here, I'd at least have plenty to eat!" Thinking about eating made her hungry again, so she ate some more of the canned peaches. She had just put them away and cleaned up when the outside door burst open.

"Doc? Kat? Whoever's here, I need you!"

Kat walked to the front in time to see Rachel dragging two boys in, each by the collar, and holding them out at arm's length. One boy had a bloody nose that was dripping all over the waiting room floor, and the other boy had some scraped fingers.

Rachel gave the boys a shove toward Kat. "They're yours. If they don't behave, feel free to hit them."

"Hit them?"

"Yes. This is the nineteenth century. It's legal here. And believe me, these two need it!" She turned around, walked out the door, and closed it behind her.

Kat took a deep breath, and said, "Okay, then. You," she pointed to the one with the bloody nose, "come with me. And you, sit down there and be quiet until I come for you. I'll only be a minute."

Kat walked into the examining room and told the boy to get on the table. "I'm going to find a rag, but until I get back, take your fingers and press against your nose here." She put his fingers where they should be, and he screamed.

183

"That hurts! I'm not doin' that! It hurts!"

"Don't press so hard, then. Just gently hold your fingers there so you don't bleed all over yourself and all over the floor."

"Who are you, anyway? Where's Doc?"

"That, young man, is none of your business. Who are *you?*"

"I'm Billy Bob." He motioned to the other room. "And he's Bobby Bill."

"Yeah, right, and I'm the Easter Bunny!" Kat disappeared from the room and reappeared holding a rag. "Okay, oh-nameless-one, hold this up to your nose. You'll have to put at least a little pressure on it to get it stopped."

"This isn't how Doc does it."

"Oh, so you've been in a fight before, have you? Well, how exactly *does* Doc do it?"

"He has me lay down, and he puts something cold on my forehead."

"Pressure works quicker. Stay where you are."

"I don't have to. You can't make me!"

Kat walked up to the boy, squinted her eyes at him, and said in her sternest ever voice, "If you get off that table, I will give you another black eye to match the one that Bobby Bill gave you."

The boy puffed up his chest, but didn't move. Kat backed slowly to the door with her eyes still narrowed and her finger pointing straight at him.

The other boy sat quietly in the waiting room. "I'm Reuben, ma'am, and he's Oscar. He told you a fib."

"Thank you, Reuben. I knew that." Kat examined his hand. It had deep scrape marks on his knuckles. "How'd you do that?"

"Hitting Oscar in the mouth, ma'am."

"So, Reuben, you started it, then."

"No, ma'am. Oscar called my mother an unmentionable name. So I gave him a good ole sockdologer, right in the nose!"

Kat walked into the examining room, checked on Oscar, got some antibiotic cream and some sticky bandages, and brought everything back in to where Reuben waited. "I thought you got that," she pointed to his scraped knuckles "from hitting him in the mouth."

"Yes, ma'am, I did. After I hit him in the nose, he said it again, so I hit him in the mouth. Then, Miss Jenkins came out and broke us up. I would have hit him again if she hadn't come outside right then."

Kat spread the cream on his knuckles, put bandages on, and stood up. "Did he hit you?"

"No, ma'am, he didn't." Reuben looked at the sticky bandage, which made Kat wonder when they were invented.

"But if he didn't hit you back, why did you keep hitting him?"

"Because he kept saying nasty things about my mother."

Exasperated, Kat shook her head. "Didn't they ever teach you 'sticks and stones can break my bones, but words can never hurt me'?"

"Yes, ma'am. But that's my bones. That verse doesn't say anything about my mother. I was defending her honor."

"Defending her honor, huh? Well, I don't know what to say about that, Reuben. But you're all fixed up, and you can go back to school now."

"What about Oscar?"

185

"He has to stay until his nose stops bleeding."

"Can I wait for him?"

"You just beat him up! Why would you want to wait for him?"

"He's my best friend."

"Reuben, you need to go back to school. I'll send Oscar along when he's stopped bleeding."

"Yes, ma'am. Thank you, ma'am. Good-bye, ma'am."

Kat shook her head as she walked back into the examining room to check on Oscar. He still sat quietly on the examining table.

"It's stopped. Can I please go now?" Oscar handed her the bloody rag.

"Yes, of course. Good-bye, Oscar."

"I'm Billy Bob," said Oscar, as he slid off the table.

"Sure ya are. Good-bye."

Oscar ran out the front door and slammed it behind him.

Glancing at her watch, she wondered how soon David would return. It wouldn't be soon enough for her.

CHAPTER FORTY-SEVEN

DOC LOOKED AT the clock when he walked inside. He still had a half hour, so he walked back to the medical section. The books he had put in the cart were still there, so he carried the ones he hadn't seen back to the seating area. Flipping through the books, he found a couple of pages that he wanted to copy and one book that he wanted to buy. He found a paper and pencil, wrote down the book he wanted to buy, and carried the other one to the copy machines that Zack had showed him.

When he pulled the dollars out of his pocket, he managed not to let the twenties fall to the floor. After copying the pages he wanted, he returned the book to the cart and walked to the door of the library. Soon, he saw Zack walking toward him, so Doc walked outside to meet him.

"Hallo, Zack."

"You ready to go already, Doc?"

"Not a very productive day today, I'm afraid."

"Some days are like that. By the way, 'hallo' isn't used here. It's 'hello' instead."

"Now I know you're hornswoggling me!" He gave Zack's arm a little push in fun.

Zack shook his head. "No, Doc, I'm not. Hello is what everybody here says. Honest. I'm not hornswoggling you—and they don't use that anymore, either!" Zack laughed. "It's almost like a new language. And you need to learn how to use 'cool' and 'awesome.' Then you'll be a regular twenty-first-century guy!"

Doc nodded his head. "Definitely time to go home, then."

"Are you leaving when we get home?"

"No, I was hoping that you'd ride out with me to conceal that trail to the cave."

"Oh, can't tonight, Doc. Madison and I have a date night tonight."

"Pardon me for asking, but why would you need a date night if you live together?"

"At home, we're always studying or something. When we go out, we can really be together and concentrate on each other. Madison and I both love our date nights. We wouldn't give them up for anything!"

"Good enough," said Doc. "I'll see what I can do on my own."

"If you can wait one more day, I can help you tomorrow morning."

Doc sighed. "I hate to stick Kat alone over there filling in for me for so long. But I guess she'll be all right. Sure, I can wait. I think it's important to fix that trail." Doc deliberately neglected to mention that he had spent most of the morning thinking about Kat, and that he couldn't wait to get back to see her.

"Well, I hope you ate enough for lunch because Madison and I leave early. There are some snacks in the cupboard that you are welcome to, though. You can eat anything that you find in there or in the refrigerator."

On the way home, Zack abruptly slowed the truck and pulled into a parking lot. "Be right back, Doc!"

"What is this place?"

"It's a drug store. I'll be back in a minute."

Doc wondered what Zack needed drugs for and thought that it was curious that they'd sell drugs in a store. Then he wondered if Kat had ever been in there, and he imagined her coming out the door smiling at him. He sighed and could hardly wait to get back to the old Red Bluff so he could see her again.

Zack came out in a minute and handed Doc a bag with something in it. "Go ahead. Open it. It's for you."

Doc stuck his hand in the bag, pulled something out, and read what was on the package. "What is a double-edged safety razor? And why would I need one? I already have a perfectly good straight edge."

"Madison is afraid you're going to slip and accidentally cut your throat."

"I'm a doctor, Zack. If I did happen to cut my throat, I'd know how to fix it!"

That made them both laugh. Doc turned the thing this way and that and looked at it from all angles. "I can try it."

"Do what you want, Doc. No pressure. Here we are, home already."

They got out of the truck and walked toward the front door. Zack picked up something by the front door. "Oh, this is yours."

Doc took the package from him. It was addressed to David Mercer, care of Zack Murphy. "Oh! My new instruments! I'm so excited!"

As soon as Doc got inside, he opened the package. "Come here, Zack! Let me try this on you! Give me your ear! Oh."

"What's wrong?"

"I can barely see anything. It had a light when Kat did it. Maybe she ordered the wrong one."

"Let me see it." Zack took it in his hand, looked at it, and opened a compartment that Doc hadn't even seen. "This is why, Doc. It needs batteries."

"What are batteries?"

"Remember I told you all about electricity? Batteries are like portable electricity. Let me look at the package. The other one, too. Okay, this one takes C batteries and this one a nine volt. I'll try to catch Madison before she passes the store." Zack pulled his phone out of his pocket and pressed the screen.

"Madison? Are you past the store yet? . . . No, I didn't forget the razor. Doc's got it. But he needs batteries for the instruments that Kat ordered for him. . . . Yeah, would you mind? He needs C batteries and one nine volt. . . . Thanks! See ya soon! . . . Miss you! . . . Bye.

"It's all set, Doc. Madison will pick up some batteries for you and bring them home. You'll be good to go, soon."

"Thanks so much, Zack. I appreciate it. You're awesome."

Zack glanced quickly up at Doc and laughed. "You're getting it, Doc! You're getting it!"

"Did I use the word correctly, Zack?"

"Perfect, Doc! Just perfect."

CHAPTER FORTY-EIGHT

Lying in bed, looking up at the tin ceiling, Kat reviewed her day. Her patients that day, the old woman and the two young boys, amused her. Then she had spent the remainder of the afternoon sitting in David's chair in front of his roll-top desk and musing about what it might be like living in this house in the nineteenth century— with David. Kat could hardly wait to get back home again, and yet another part of her could hardly wait to see him again.

There was something about him that was different from any other man she'd ever met. Of course, you ninny! He's from the nineteenth century! She chided herself, but it made her smile. No, it was more than that. David had the enthusiasm of a child, the dependability of an adult, and the serenity of mind that came from someone who was at peace with who they were. Yes, David was all of that. And that's why she liked him. And also why she didn't want to like him. Feelings like that could lead her to places that she didn't want to go. Places that might cause her pain, like the pain she felt when Billy was killed. Kat didn't ever want to feel like that again. She sighed and returned to thoughts about her day.

When dinner time came around—or supper as they called it here—she walked over to the hotel and was surprised to find that Josiah and Jenna were there, too. The meal started pleasantly enough, eating the delicious food and enjoying the feeling of being with family, but then it progressed to something that Kat didn't even want to be a part of. Granny and Eliza had decided that it would be better for Jenna and Josiah to stay at the hotel rather than staying in Josiah's small room at the jail.

"How can you even consider giving birth in a jail? What kind of start to life is that for a child?" asked Granny. "Duh, I was born in a jail," Granny said in a voice imitating a child.

But Josiah and Jenna were having none of it. They insisted they were comfortable at the jail, and that's where they wanted to stay.

"Then why are you staying at the ranch house now?" asked Eliza.

"Because the ranch house is *more* comfortable," conceded Jenna.

Josiah's objections, though, were purely practical. He wanted to know what would happen if someone needed the sheriff in the middle of the night. How would they find him?

Granny suggested a sign, but Eliza said that as quick as word traveled in Red Bluff, the whole town would know the sheriff was staying at the hotel before they even moved in. Everyone laughed at that, but agreed that it was probably true.

Josiah didn't think that he could respond quickly

enough if he was in an upstairs room. Samuel said that they could clean out the large storage area under the stairs, and make it comfortable for them.

Then Jenna asked Josiah to help her outside to the outhouse. When they returned, Josiah asked to see the storage room. He came back nodding his head. "Okay, here's the thing. That room is large enough to put a composting toilet in the far corner, away from the bed. Would you let us do that?"

Eliza and Samuel quickly agreed, everyone hugged, and it was settled. When the conversation turned in that direction, Kat had thought that they had asked her to be there to help convince Jenna. But they had never asked her to speak, and eventually she decided that they wanted her there because she was family. That thought made her take a deep breath, scrunch up her mouth, and wipe the tears from her eyes. Family. It had been so long since she enjoyed that kind of familiar camaraderie. She liked the feeling.

Kat looked around the bedroom, but it was now too dark to see. She wondered what it would be like if David was part of that family, too. That gave her a funny feeling in her stomach. She had shunned any kind of emotional involvement for so long that she couldn't believe she was even considering it. But she was. She really was. Now all it depended on was if David felt the same way. While she hoped he did, she also realized that if he didn't, life would be a lot easier. And then she fell asleep.

CHAPTER FORTY-NINE

DOC WOKE UP early ready to get the day going. He wanted to get the trail fixed and be on his way home. He was especially eager to try out his new instruments on a real patient, and he was even more eager to see Kat. Was she as beautiful as he remembered? Doc smiled and thought that she was probably more beautiful than he remembered. How was she doing taking care of the town, he wondered. Was it too much for her? Should he have not left her alone? The thoughts made him even more motivated to get home.

Doc thought it was strange that he didn't hear Zack or Madison moving about. They were always up before him. Where were they? Well, if they weren't up yet, it didn't make sense for him to get up. He didn't know how to use those twenty-first-century gadgets in the kitchen. If he tried, he'd probably blow the place up.

That brought Kat back to mind. How, he wondered, was Kat coping with his nineteenth-century instruments and medical practices. He hoped she wasn't sneaking in some twenty-first-century tricks and scaring his patients. They'd think he'd left them with a witch doctor, and maybe they wouldn't even trust *him* anymore! They'd ride him out on a rail!

No, Kat wouldn't do that. At least, he hoped she wouldn't do that. That Kat, though, she definitely had a mind of her own and her own way of doing things. He liked that strength in her, admired it. That day they had spent together was so easy, so comfortable, it was almost as if they belonged together. And he liked that thought, and the more he got used to the thought of not being alone anymore, the more he liked it. The more he thought about Kat and him being together, the more he wanted it to happen. And he wanted it to happen soon, which meant time was a-wasting while he was stuck here in the twenty-first century when Kat was in the nineteenth. Listening, he still didn't hear any movement in the house.

He stood up, stretched, and quickly got dressed. Then he walked to the bathroom. Realizing that he had left his razor and the new razor that Zack had bought him back in his room, he returned to retrieve them. Back in front of the mirror, he decided to try out the new razor that he had unpackaged the night before. The ease of it astonished him. Another twenty-first-century invention that was, in Zack's words, awesome! When he finished, he ran his hand over his face and discovered that it didn't shave as close as his straight edge. He looked at himself in the mirror. He was about to let it go, when he remembered that he would see Kat today for the first time in a few days, and he wanted to be completely clean-shaven. So, he got out his straight edge, and began re-shaving his face.

"What are you doing, Doc? I bought you the new razor. Why are you using that one?" asked Zack, peering into the open door.

"I need to remember to close that door when I shave! That razor didn't shave close enough."

"Maybe not as close as a straight razor, but it's close enough."

"Not always," said Doc and winked at Zack.

"Oh. *Oh!*"

Doc figured that Zack walked away from the door so fast because he was embarrassed, which made Doc laugh. But he didn't know what possessed him to even say such a thing to Zack. The twenty-first century was having a strange effect on him, and he was getting more and more impatient to go back to his own time.

He was in his room putting away both razors when he heard Zack's voice again, calling out from the other room. Doc stepped out of his room and walked through the hall and toward the kitchen.

"Breakfast is ready. Sorry, I forgot to tell you yesterday that we sleep in on the weekends." Zack put the plate in front of Doc.

"No problem, Zack, I'm just anxious to get home. I'm worried about what Kat might have had to put up with while I've been gone."

"I'm sure she's fine," said Madison. "My mom can handle anything."

"Or that's what she wants you to believe," said Doc, raising his eyebrows at Madison.

She stopped, tilted her head, and looked at him. "You're right, Doc, you're absolutely right."

After breakfast, Doc paid Zack and Madison the money that he owed. Then he walked out to the barn, saddled Crackle, and attached one bag behind the saddle. He mounted up and put on the backpack that was hanging on the edge of the stall. Then he and Zack rode out, carrying a rake and a shovel with them. When they arrived at the trail turnoff point, they surveyed the situation.

"I think we ought to cover up the trail completely for at least twenty feet, till it curves around that bush up there. What do you think, Zack?"

"I think that's a great idea, Doc. Then we can work on the new trail afterward."

They dismounted and, Zack with the shovel and Doc with the rake, covered the trail so well that no one would ever know there had ever been a trail there. They walked back down to the main trail and surveyed their work.

"It's perfect, Zack. Great job!"

"Now let's figure out how to hide the new trail—and where to put it."

"Let's ride back down the trail away from this spot. We want people to forget there was ever a trail here."

"Good idea. I know a good spot." They rode for several minutes before Zack stopped. "What do you think of this, Doc?"

Doc rode Crackle over to where Zack had stopped. It was a dry wash, lined with sand, but about four feet from the main trail, the sand turned to large pieces of gravel, and then a little farther up, turned to larger rocks. "Let's get off and walk it. I don't want the animals getting stuck up there."

He got off and started walking up the wash. Zack followed. They walked on the larger rocks for only a few feet when the trail ended at a large boulder. Doc looked down the way they had come. "If we could make this work, Zack, it would be perfect."

"I think if we dig up these two little bushes—let's get the shovel and rake, and walk the way back to the other trail."

Forty-five minutes later, the new trail was finished, with the two little bushes transplanted in the middle of the old trail to make it look even more natural. The two men felt satisfied with the way it looked. They sat on their mounts from the main trail and looked up at their handiwork. "From here, it looks like the wash leads to a dead end."

"Which is exactly how we want it to look, Zack. Great choice! Thanks for helping me do this—or I think it was more like I helped you!"

Zack laughed. "No problem, Doc. That trail to the cave being so obvious like that could have hurt all of us. I remember Sarah saying that after she was rescued from those scalawags, she was afraid that they would find the trail here and come after her. It is a risk. Always."

"But I think we just made the risk smaller. And I'm good with that."

"Oh, no, Doc!"

"What is it, Zack?" asked Doc, concerned.

"We need to cover the trail on the other side of the cave, too!"

"You're right, Zack. We do need to do that. But not today. I need to get back.

"Thanks, Zack, and thanks for letting me stay with you and Madison. Good-bye!" Doc waved and urged Crackle up the new trail they had just created.

CHAPTER FIFTY

KAT WOKE UP wondering where David was. Shouldn't he be back by now? Did something bad happen to him in the twenty-first century so he couldn't get back? Stop it, Kat, she told herself. Had something happened, Zack or Madison would have come back here and let her know. All is well. He's having himself a good ole time, while she filled in for him. But she hoped he'd return soon. Not just because she wanted to be relieved of duty, but because she really wanted to see him.

There was a part of her that felt guilty that she wanted him to take his job back. She was a nurse, why would taking care of sick and injured people make her feel this way? Kat knew why. It was because she was limited to archaic techniques to cure them, and she wasn't comfortable with that. The newer instruments, medicines, and methods *already* existed—which was why she struggled with not being able to use them. What she had to keep reminding herself was that they didn't exist *here*. Well, whatever, because she had gotten along fine so far, and with any luck, Doc would be home soon.

Kat walked downstairs to light the wood stove for

coffee. Thinking ahead, she also prepared the coffee, and then started back up the stairs. She'd never before minded Rachel, but she also had never had her forced upon her without escape like this, either. When she reached the top of the stairs, she heard Rachel down below announcing her arrival. Ignoring her, Kat washed her face and brushed her teeth in the bowl of water that she had changed the evening before. Then when she was good and ready, she slowly walked downstairs and into the kitchen to face Rachel.

"Hi, Kat! Thanks for starting the fire and making the coffee. You're getting the hang of this now."

"Thanks, Rachel," Kat said without enthusiasm.

"So you think you might want to stay here?" Rachel poured them each a cup of coffee.

"I doubt it."

"You doubt it! So there's a chance, then! Way to go, Kat! You'll really love it here."

"Rachel, I never said I was moving here or even that I was considering moving here. It was a very noncommittal 'I doubt it' so why are you getting so excited?"

"Because you didn't say no, Kat! And you've always been a decisive person. I think you've decided already! You've moving here, aren't you?"

Kat stood up slowly trying to maintain her sanity. "Rachel, you are officially impossible. Good-bye." She took one more sip of the still hot coffee and walked briskly from the kitchen and up the stairs to the safety of her room. Five minutes later, she heard Rachel leave without a word. Finally, thought Kat.

She proceeded back downstairs and into the kitchen, where she finished off the last of the canned peaches. Kat thought she could definitely get used to the food here—no preservatives, no GMOs, everything was organic and all the animals were grass fed and natural. That was one thing about the future that was more of a struggle than the nineteenth century. Food was still pristine back in the nineteenth century. You didn't have to make an effort to eat naturally, you just ate, and it was already natural. She wouldn't mind at all living in a place like that. Well, here was like that. So she guessed that meant that she wouldn't mind living here.

Her thoughts were interrupted by someone rushing in the front door. Kat's first thought was that she hoped it wasn't Rachel. Then she heard a young male voice say, "Doc! Doc! We need you! My brother fell out of the same tree and broke his arm again!"

Kat ran downstairs in time to see an entire family in the waiting room: two young boys, a woman holding a baby, and a man carrying a boy with some kind of cast on his arm. They were all agitated, and the boy with the broken arm was crying hysterically. "Quick. Bring him in here." Kat walked into the examining room, ready to prepare him for a quick x-ray before setting his arm. For some reason, she walked into the kitchen thinking she would find the machine there—but all she found was a smoking wood stove, a dry sink, and two free-standing wooden cupboards. Oh, no, thought Kat. What do I do now?

She turned around and walked to the boy who was now sitting on the examining table, still crying. First, she had to get the old cast off. Part of it was soft, like it had been in water. What was it made of, anyway? No time for that now, the kid wouldn't stop crying. Using a heavy scissors from one of Doc's drawers, Kat finally managed to get the cast completely off. Then she started palpating the arm. The boy screamed, struggled out of his father's arms, and ran into the waiting room with his mother and two brothers.

His father and brothers brought him back, and then the three of them held the boy on the examining table. Kat went back to palpating the arm. The boy screamed again and struggled to get free. Now I have to start again, thought Kat. Without an x-ray, she had to be doubly sure she would get the bone in the correct position. As soon as she put her fingers on the boy's arm, he screamed.

"I'm sorry, but I have to do this to make sure I set it correctly."

"The other doctor didn't do it that way," said the man who had carried the boy in.

Kat exhaled forcefully and said, "The other doctor is not here right now." She decided she would go for it— because without an x-ray, she had to. There was no other choice. So she quickly grabbed the boy's arm and before she had a chance to put the broken bone together, the boy escaped again and ran to his mother.

"Don't let her touch me! It hurts! I don't want her to do it! Get the other doctor! I won't go back in the other room with her! She's mean and awful! I won't go."

Kat, exasperated and feeling like crying herself, said, "I can do this. I just need to get the bone in place, and it shouldn't hurt anymore. I can do this." She wondered if she was trying to convince herself she could, because at that moment, she had absolutely no confidence at all in her ability to set that boy's arm.

"No, Mommy! Don't make me! Don't make me! She's horrible! She hurt me! Don't make me."

Kat stepped forward toward the woman and the boy,

and he screamed again. The woman tried to comfort him. And then Doc walked in the door, just as the boy let out an especially loud ear-splitting scream.

Kat watched wordlessly as Doc came in and handled the situation. First he took off the backpack and put it down on the floor next to the bag he had been carrying. Then he took the boy by the hand and lifted him up to the examining table. The boy's father and two brothers accompanied him. The boy looked up at Doc, and with a tear-stained face, said, "I'll let you work on me, doctor. I'll be good now." Kat watched as Doc quickly set the bone and began putting on another cast. She knew she should watch and learn, but her heart wasn't in it. Silently, she slipped out the front door and headed over to the saloon. She wasn't a drinker, but this seemed like a good time to start.

CHAPTER FIFTY-ONE

"KAT!" JENNA'S FRIEND, Sarah, had come to the old Red Bluff to play the piano and sing, and had ended up married to the saloon owner, Matthew.

Kat hugged her. "Good to see you, Sarah. How is everything? You happy here?"

Sarah nodded. "Ecstatic. Matthew is the best husband ever, and life here is—you know, simple. I like it.

"I heard you're in town for Jenna's birth. How are you adjusting?"

"Fine, just fine." Kat looked away and then looked back at Sarah. "No, Sarah, not fine at all. I just totally flubbed a simple broken arm."

"How would you do it, anyway, without an x-ray machine?"

"Exactly! I didn't know, but luckily David returned from," Kat motioned to the side with her head, "there, and handled it for me. I came here to get myself drunk."

"Who's David?"

"Oh, I forgot. You know. Doc."

"So Doc's name is David, hmmm. Ah, whatever.

Listen, Kat, I didn't think you drank."

"This is a good time to start."

"Matthew! Sarsaparilla for my friend, Kat!" And then to Kat, Sarah said, "Kat, you don't need a drink, you need a friend."

Kat looked at her and crinkled her brow. "You're right, Sarah. That's exactly what I need."

Sarah had been sitting at the piano, but now she stood up and took Kat's arm. "Come on, we can go in the back."

Kat followed Sarah. As she walked by the bar, Sarah's handsome husband, Matthew, handed her a glass. "Thank you."

They walked into a room off the back of the bar. It had a wood stove, a table, and some wooden cupboards. They sat at the table.

"I didn't even want to be here, Sarah." It wasn't like Kat to confess anything to anyone, but right now, she needed a sounding board, and Sarah was it. "But you know how stubborn Jenna can be. So here I am."

"And how did Doc find out about—you know."

"Oh, that. Before I decided to move here to help Jenna, I figured the more Doc knew about the future of medicine, the safer everyone in town would be. So I gave him some current medical books."

Sarah laughed. "Kat, you didn't!"

Kat nodded. "Yeah, I did. And of course when he figured it all out, he insisted on going there to see everything himself. So I took him."

"I'm sure he was amazed like everyone else. So are you falling victim to the nineteenth-century-man syndrome?"

"The what?"

"These nineteenth-century men have something special about them that twenty-first-century men can't compete with. So my question is, have you started to like Doc more than you thought you would?"

"No, of course not." Kat looked at the table and didn't meet Sarah's eyes.

Sarah bent her head and tilted it so she could look up at Kat's face. "Are you sure?"

Kat slapped the table top with her hand. "Oh, all right. I find him interesting."

Sarah laughed and nodded. "I don't think, in all the years I've known you, that I've heard you say that about any man before."

"Well, don't let it get around. I don't plan on staying long enough to see if I'm right or wrong."

"What if Jenna's baby is late?"

Kat looked at Sarah. "Then I'll probably be in trouble."

Noise in the saloon distracted Kat—loud voices that sounded familiar. "She's back there." Kat heard someone say. A second later, Edward, Granny's husband, appeared.

"Kat! Granny needs you!"

Kat jumped up and ran into the saloon. Granny sat in a chair by the door, looking pale. Kat ran to her.

"Granny? What's wrong?"

Granny didn't speak. It appeared that she was having trouble breathing.

"She's been having trouble breathing off and on and has had some spells," Edward said.

Granny glared at him. She caught her breath and croaked out, "You promised you wouldn't tell!"

"Old woman, if I keep my promise and you die, then

what good will it do me?"

Just then, the swinging doors opened and Doc strode in, with his new stethoscope around his neck. "What's this I hear about you getting dizzy?" He looked at Kat and offered her the stethoscope.

"No, you," said Kat, still staring at Granny.

Doc knelt down and put the stethoscope to Granny's chest. He nodded. Moved the stethoscope around and nodded again. He looked at Kat. "Slow. It's too slow and uneven."

Kat reached out her hand, and Doc gave her the stethoscope. She placed it on Granny's chest. "He's right, Granny. You have an irregular heartbeat. You need to see a cardiologist."

That got Granny going. "If you think I'm going to carry this sorry ole butt back *there* just to see a doctor, you're crazy! This is my home now, and this is where I stay!"

"Granny, this isn't an option. You have to go. It's dangerous not to."

"I'm not going. Edward, take me home now."

"Granny, this isn't the first time it's happened, is it?" Kat had her hands on her hips looking at Granny.

"That's none of your business, granddaughter. I'm fine now. That's all that matters."

"Granny," Doc said, "is that how you got hurt before? You got dizzy and dropped that big bowl that cut you?"

Granny, not answering, folded her arms across her chest and looked at the floor. "Edward, take me home, *now*."

"Kat. What do you mean it's dangerous?" Edward put one hand on Granny's shoulder and looked at Kat.

"She could have a heart attack or a stroke."

"What?" he asked.

"Oh, a heart attack means that something happens to the heart. It has an attack and doesn't function properly. People die from that. And a stroke is a . . . a . . . David, can you help me here?" Kat looked at Doc for support.

"I believe what Kat is describing is apoplexy, Edward."

"Oh, no," said Edward. "If they can do something in the place you come from to fix that, you have to go."

"I'm not going anywhere, Edward. This is my home now, and this is where I stay. Now take me home, you old coot, before I dump you for some strong, young thing."

Edward bent down and put his face an inch from Granny's face. "Listen, you old biddy. If you think you can just die on me, or have an apoplexy, you're wrong. Taking care of some infirm old weakling is not in my plans. You will return from whence you came, and you will get yourself fixed. That's that!" He stood up and crossed his arms over his chest.

"Granny, it's not a big deal. They'll give you some tests, and probably prescribe some pills for you." Kat patted Granny's hand.

"And have to be dependent on pills all my life—and having to return *there* to get them? Nothing doing!"

"Granny, they might be able to give you a pacemaker. That way you wouldn't have to take pills. How about that?" asked Kat.

"I'd still have to go back *there*," said Granny, but in a softer voice.

"Just once." Kat knew that with a pacemaker, Granny should return for checkups, but she wasn't going to tell that to Granny now. "*I'll* go with you."

"No! I don't want you to go with me! You don't live here. You don't understand how I feel about living here. I need someone who understands life here and why I love it." She looked at Edward. "And it can't be him because he doesn't want to go."

"I'll go if you want me to, dear," said Edward. "You know I will."

"No, you don't have to," said Granny.

Doc stepped forward. "*I'll* go with you, Granny. I live here; I know what you love about it here; I've been *there*, and I can accompany you."

"I was hoping you'd say that," said Granny, looking straight at Doc.

CHAPTER FIFTY-TWO

DOC COULD TELL that Kat felt bad. He could see her blinking her eyes and tightening her mouth. But she still stayed by Granny, trying not to show how hurt she was.

Kat felt her pockets. "I don't have my cell. If I had my cell, I could call the cardiologist today and arrange everything. I'll ride over there now."

"No," Granny said. "You will not go all the way there on my account. It's not necessary."

"The sooner the better, Granny," said Kat.

"Kat, come here," said Sarah.

"Sarah, I'm in the middle of something here. Can't you see that?" Kat said sternly.

"Kat, come here," said Sarah more forcefully.

Kat, taken aback, followed Sarah up to the bar. They were too far away for Doc to hear anything, but he saw Sarah give something to Kat. And then Kat returned.

"Okay, here's the deal. When you got hurt, Granny, Zack called me from right outside—" She leaned down and whispered in Granny's ear, but it was loud enough for Doc to hear "the cave." Kat picked her head up and continued, "So I'll go there now. It won't be all the way.

It won't take me long. And you'll be okay with that. Right?"

"With everybody hanging all over me like this, I guess it will have to be," said Granny. "Do you need me here any longer, or can my husband take me home now?"

Kat leaned over and kissed Granny. "I'll make the appointment for Monday, Granny. Be ready. Oh! She can't ride a horse like this."

"Of course I can ride a horse! I've been riding horses since before—"

Doc interrupted. "We can take my cart—the one Sarah used to transport Zack when he was sick. You'll be okay with that, right, Granny?"

"I suppose so. Can I go home now? Please?"

Edward helped her up and put an arm around her, and they walked through the swinging doors together. A second later, Granny peeked her head back in. "I'm not staying overnight. And don't try to trick me, either! I'm not staying apart from my husband for even one night!"

Doc saw Kat nod, but it didn't look genuine. He hoped that Granny hadn't noticed that.

"Are you okay, Kat? You look upset." Doc put his hand on her arm.

"Thanks for coming with your stethoscope, Doc. I appreciate that."

"Samuel came to get me. Apparently, someone thought they had seen you come in here, but Granny didn't believe it, so she sent Samuel to get me. The family with the little boy had just left."

"Oh."

Doc realized too late that Kat didn't want to be reminded of what had happened earlier. "How about if I ride out with you to keep you company?"

"If you want to," Kat said, shrugging.

"I'll get our mounts." Doc squeezed her arm and walked out the swinging doors.

Striding quickly to the livery, he called to Ezra when he got there. "Ezra, will you saddle up Kat's horse, please? I'll take care of Crackle." Doc brushed and saddled the mule, and by the time he was ready, Kat's horse was saddled. He walked them both back to the saloon, and left them in front to get Kat.

She walked out of the saloon before he had a chance to go in. "I'm ready." She sounded tired. Very tired.

"Do you want help up, Kat?"

She shook her head no and mounted up. Doc climbed onto Crackle. They rode in silence for several minutes.

"Did Sarah give you her phone?"

"Yes. I can't believe she keeps it here. For no reason! She even has a solar charger to keep it charged all the time!"

"What's a solar charger?"

"It's a little device that she leaves out in the sun that creates enough electricity to run the phone. Look, here we are."

Riding through the cave, Doc thought he heard Kat sniffling. "Are you okay, Kat?"

They emerged on the other side, and Doc saw tears in Kat's eyes. She held the phone in front of her and started pressing it. "I can't believe that Granny would go with you and not with me. I can't believe that."

Kat put the phone to her ear. "Zack? You home? . . . Can you do me a favor? Look up Dr. Galinski for me, will you? . . . Yes, the cardiologist. Cool, thanks." Kat pressed on the phone again and then put it to her ear.

Doc heard what she was saying to the doctor, but he didn't understand all the words. It sounded like it was going well, though, and Granny would get the appointment. Apparently in the twenty-first century, appointments were necessary to see doctors. Doc was glad that it wasn't that way in the nineteenth century—it was more easy going, more natural. More his style.

Kat hung up the phone. "It's all set then. He'll be expecting you and Granny at ten o'clock. Is that all right?"

"Of course it is, Kat, of course it is."

"I hate this!" said Kat. "I hate this! I hate that Granny chose you over me, and I hate that I couldn't take care of that kid today. I should go home and never come back! I'm useless here!"

Doc put his arm around her the best he could with him and Kat both on their mounts. "Come on. Let's go home now."

CHAPTER FIFTY-THREE

NORMALLY, KAT WOULD have shoved his arm away and told him that she could handle it herself. But his arm around her felt strangely comforting, and it made her feel better. She leaned into him as best she could while staying in the saddle.

Five minutes later, still in front of the cave, Doc said, "You ready to go back now, Kat?"

Kat sighed heavily. "Not really."

Doc tightened his grip on her shoulder. "We can stay here as long as you want."

Minutes went by. She could feel the warmth of his hand through her clothes. It felt good. Kat felt like she could stay right like that, leaning into him, for a very long time. Instead, she straightened up and said, "Let's go."

Doc let her enter the cave first, and he followed. Kat felt like she could burst into tears at any minute, and she could hardly wait to get out of the cave. When they emerged on the other side, she trotted to the main road and waited for Doc to catch up. As soon as she looked at him, he put his arm around her again, and she relaxed

214

into the warmth of it. She felt like he really cared about her, and she liked that feeling—she hadn't known it in so long, so very long. Sighing softly, she leaned into him again, sitting at the edge of her saddle. If Paisley spooked at anything on her left side, Kat would either be on the ground or in David's lap. But Paisley was a solid old girl, and Kat couldn't even remember the last time she spooked at anything.

They passed the Red Bluff, Colorado, sign and Doc squeezed her shoulder and whispered, "It will be all right, Kat. It will be fine."

For the next few minutes, listening to the animals' hooves on the hard-packed road and feeling David beside her, Kat was at absolute peace. She couldn't have asked for another thing in the world. And although her emotions were roiling just beneath the surface, for right now, she felt peace. And it felt good. It felt very good.

They rode like that, cuddled up, until the town was up ahead. After a few more paces, Doc took his arm away. It had been there for so long that it felt almost a part of her, and when he took it away, it stunned her so much that she gasped. She looked at him and couldn't stop the fat tears from rolling down her face.

"You don't want to be seen with me?" she asked him.

"Kat, no! It's nothing like that. I know how private you are, and I didn't think you'd want people thinking something that wasn't true."

Kat shook her head from side to side while the tears slid down her face. "You're embarrassed to be seen with the likes of me. I get it." And she kicked Paisley to get her going. She never kicked Paisley; she couldn't even remember the last time she had. More than ten years ago, to be sure. And Paisley, not accustomed to being kicked, took off quickly, and Kat had to rein her in to keep her from a dead run. As they cantered away from Doc, Kat heard him say, "I'd be proud to be seen with you, Kat. I think you're awesome!"

Awesome? Did he really just say she was awesome? If the situation wasn't so tragic, she would be laughing hysterically. As it was, she dropped the reins on Paisley's neck and clapped both hands to her face. Paisley slowed, but kept up a fast walk. And Kat let her be. And she cried, and she cried, and she cried.

CHAPTER FIFTY-FOUR

As Doc approached the livery, he could see Kat running down the street. He felt bad and wondered what he could have done differently. Probably just asked her if she minded being seen with his arm about her shoulders. That would have been the smart thing to do, he chided himself. Stopping just inside the entrance to the livery, Doc dismounted. Ezra had already unsaddled Kat's mare and was brushing her down.

"Ezra? Can you take care of Crackle, too?"

"Sure thing, Doc. Is Kat all right?"

"She will be, Ezra. She will be."

Doc led Crackle into his stall and took his bridle off. Then he walked down the street. He didn't know where Kat would have gone, but he would find her. Should he check the hotel first, or would she have returned to the saloon? Something told him to go home first.

When he walked into the house, he heard something upstairs. A sniffling. It was here. Kat had come here. To him. He climbed up the stairs and looked into her room. She lay on the bed with her back facing the door, and at the side of the bed, was her backpack, already

217

packed.

She hadn't come home to him, she had come back here to pack her things. He shook his head at his own arrogance, and then walked into the room. "Kat? Kat, I'm sorry." He put his hand on her shoulder.

Kat moved her shoulder away from his touch. "Leave me alone. I'm only here because I can't go back to the hotel looking like this. I need some time to get myself together and then I'll get out of your hair, and you'll never have to put up with me again."

"Kat, please." He put his hand on her shoulder again.

This time, she turned toward him. Her face was bright red, and tears streamed down her cheeks, but he could still see the rage in her eyes. "I said, leave me alone!" She screamed it at him, and he backed quietly out the door to leave her alone.

Her rage shocked Doc so much that he walked into his own room and patted his face with cold water from the bowl. He shook off the feeling and retreated downstairs. Sitting in the easy chair in the waiting room, he thought about Kat. She was one of the strongest women he had ever known, and now he knew that she was also one of the most sensitive. But she always hid her sensitive side from everyone. Why would she do that? What was she afraid of?

Doc puttered around downstairs waiting for Kat to come down. But she never did. Finally, he walked up to the hotel for supper. After he finished, he asked them to prepare a plate that he could take back with him. When he arrived back home, he walked upstairs and looked in at Kat. She was still faced away from the door, but he could tell she was still crying, because she was making sniffling sounds and her shoulders were gently shaking.

"Kat," he said in a soft voice, "I'm leaving supper here for you. You need something to eat." He put the plate next to the pitcher and bowl of water, and then he returned downstairs.

Doc wanted to read his new books, but he had brought the backpack upstairs and didn't want to disturb Kat again by going up there. So he decided to mosey on up to the saloon and have a beer.

He took a table in the back—it was the one that Zack used to sit at to read—and he sat down. Sarah came over. "Doc! Are you ready for your monthly beer?"

Doc laughed. "That's about it, isn't it, Sarah? Yes, I'll try not to drink it too fast so it will last me another month!"

"Good enough. I'll be right back."

Sarah used to only do the singing in the bar, but since Zack left and Rawlins started acting like a deputy, she and Matthew didn't have anyone who could wait on the tables. She was good natured about it, though, and sometimes she would even sing while she served drinks. Doc liked her.

Sarah brought him the beer and whispered into his ear, "Thanks for taking care of Granny. She can be a handful!"

Doc nodded and sipped the beer. He hoped that Sarah would have time to play the piano while he was there. As if answering his silent request, Sarah sat down at the piano and began to sing "Red River Valley." One of his favorites. She sang several more songs, and then Doc was finished with his beer, so he quietly left the saloon and walked back home.

He went out the back door to use the necessary and thought about how wonderful it would be to have a flush toilet. It was so convenient! When he came back in, he slowly made his way up the stairs, trying not to make any noise. Walking over to Kat's room, he looked in. She slept peacefully. He was never sure what made him do it, but he stepped over to the bed, scooped Kat up in his arms, carried her into his bedroom, and gently put her down on his bed. Then he lay down beside her, cradled her in his arms, and fell asleep.

CHAPTER FIFTY-FIVE

KAT AWOKE WHEN the sun began streaming though the windows. She felt David's body still wrapped around hers. They both still had their clothes on. The previous night, when he had carried her into his room, she woke briefly, but was too emotionally exhausted to fight it. And sleeping next to him like that, feeling his warmth and his arms around her all night, comforted her so much that she almost felt healed.

Doc moved, and Kat quickly shut her eyes. She didn't want him to know she was awake. He slowly unwrapped himself from her and got out of bed. Then he walked to her side of the bed and said in a whisper, "Kat, I'd be proud to have you by my side anytime. I honestly do think that you're awesome!" And he kissed her gently on the lips and walked out of the room.

Kat was stunned. She had never expected anything like *that*. Wow. But what happened yesterday and last night were more indicators that she should not be with a man. Any man. Even David. It just wasn't right for her. She and Billy were wonderful together, and now he was gone. For some reason that she couldn't figure out, that was to be her only love in this life, and she had resigned herself to that. Besides, she felt so embarrassed about what happened last night. She was so much of an emotional wreck that David had to rescue her and cuddle her all night like he would a scared child. How embarrassing!

The front door of the house opened. A voice that Kat recognized as Rachel, said, "Doc! Kat! Anybody here?"

David's voice called out, "I'll be right down, Rachel." Then she heard him walking down the stairs.

"Where's Kat?" asked Rachel in a voice unlike her own.

Kat held her breath. Regardless of what ever did or didn't happen with David, she did not want Rachel to know she was upstairs.

"Oh, now that I'm back, I didn't need her filling in for me, anymore."

Thank you, David, thought Kat. I don't need my personal flaws and emotional outbursts spread around town. She listened for Rachel's response to what David had said, but they had already walked into the kitchen. Now was her chance! She'd have to sneak downstairs and out the door before either of them saw her. Crawling out of bed as silently as possible, she tiptoed to her room to retrieve her backpack. When the floor creaked, she'd stop momentarily and then move forward again. With her backpack over her shoulder, she stole down the stairs as silently as she could. Opening the front door a fraction of an inch at a time, she managed to slip out and close it the same way with a minimum of sound.

Finally out on the street, she felt immense relief and walked briskly to the hotel. When she opened the door, Granny was behind the front desk. "Oh!" she said.

"Where you been all night? Out Katin' around?" Then she howled with laughter.

Kat, still feeling hurt from the day before, ignored her and ran up the stairs to her room. She took off all her clothes, climbed under the covers, and fell into a peaceful sleep. Until five minutes later when she heard a pounding on her door.

"Kat? Are you okay in there? Don't be so sensitive, Kat. I didn't mean to tease you about you and the doctor."

"It's all right, but there *is* no me and the doctor. Just leave me alone."

"And I'm sorry I didn't want you to go with me back *there*, but I honestly didn't think you would understand."

"It's all right, Granny. I just want to be left alone right now."

"You should come out and be with the family. It would make you feel better."

Kat sat up in bed and screamed. "I'd feel better if you'd just leave me alone! Now go!" Kat heard Granny say something that might have been an expletive and might have been nineteenth-century jargon, and then Kat heard Granny's footsteps fade away down the hall.

No matter what she tried, she couldn't fall asleep again. Thoughts kept popping up in her mind. Thoughts that she didn't want to pay attention to, but they wouldn't go away. David was warm and genuinely kind to her. Why would she push him away? Why not let herself be happy with a man for once? She didn't have to punish herself for what happened to Billy. The war killed him, she didn't. Time to let go of that pain and allow happiness back into her life. After agonizing over her feelings for David for more than an hour, Kat finally came to the conclusion that yes, she was ready. She'd stay in bed awhile longer and then get up, get dressed, and go back to David's. Maybe she'd even kiss *him* on the lips.

CHAPTER FIFTY-SIX

DOC COULDN'T WAIT for Rachel to leave so he could go up and check on Kat. He thought he had heard her moving around and had maybe even heard the front door open and close, but he wasn't sure. But since there was no school that day, Rachel stayed longer than usual. When Rachel finally let herself out the front door, Doc hurried upstairs and looked around. Kat was gone. Her backpack was gone. There was no sign of her at all.

Doc's mood drooped. He had wanted so much to talk to her and tell her that everything would be okay. And he wanted to tell her—when she was awake—that he really did care for her. She meant the world to him, and it was time for him to come out and say it. Either she would respond or she wouldn't, but Doc had to find out. He couldn't wait. Because behind Kat's rough exterior and sometimes rude ways of handling things, he felt that he and she had truly connected. And he didn't want to let that go.

The front door opened, and Doc hoped it was Kat. But instead, it was Kat's sister, Jenna. "Hallo, Jenna. How is everything?"

"Can I talk to you, Doc? I'm a little worried."

"Sure, Jenna, come on in." He led her into the examining room and had her sit on a chair. "What is it, dear?"

"I'm not sure if I'm imagining this or not, but it seems like the baby isn't moving as much as he was. Can you check on him to make sure everything is okay?"

"Certainly, Jenna. But if you're not sure, it might be just nerves." Doc picked up his new stethoscope and showed it to Jenna. "Look at this. Kat ordered it for me. Fresh from the twenty-first century!"

Jenna laughed. "Nice."

Doc knelt in front of her and put the stethoscope on her belly. Moving it around, he nodded his head. Then he put his hand on her, where the stethoscope was, and felt all around. "Jenna, everything appears to be fine. The baby sounds normal. Is he still kicking?"

"Oh, yes, that he is. It doesn't seem as often, though."

"If he's still kicking and everything sounds normal, I think maybe it's new-mother nervousness. I do think it's getting close, though."

Jenna's eyes brightened. "You do?"

Doc nodded. "I think that baby is getting ready." The front door opened, and Doc said, "I'll be right back. Let me see who this is."

He walked to the waiting room. Rachel came in through the door with an unusual expression on her face. "Doc, I wanted to give you this." She grabbed him, and before he could pull away, she had planted her lips on his. He put his hands on her shoulders and began to push her away, when the front door opened. It was Kat. She took one look at Rachel and Doc, and with a look of horror on her face, slammed the door shut again.

Doc pushed Rachel away and stepped back. "Rachel, this isn't appropriate. You're almost half my age and we are friends. Just friends."

Rachel laughed. "Oh, Doc, I'm a little bit older than half your age, a lot more, actually. And friendship is a good start for a *deeper* relationship." She took a step toward him.

Doc held out his arms to stop her from getting any closer. "No, Rachel. Now please leave. I have business to take care of." He pointed to the door. "Now."

"Oh, wow, okay, *sorry*," Rachel said and walked out the door.

Doc walked back into the room with Jenna. He leaned against the examining table, took one look at her, and said, "Oh, dear."

"Wow," said Jenna. "I had no idea that Rachel felt that way about you. Looks like you didn't, either."

Doc shook his head and looked at the ground. "Did you see your sister peek her head in the door just as Rachel kissed me? Oh, dear. What a fix!"

"Doc, I'd like to say that she'd understand, but my sister is notorious for *not* understanding. I'm sorry, Doc."

He looked up at Jenna. "It's all right. If it's meant to be, it will be. If not, not. Anyway, you're fine, young lady, and soon you'll be bringing a healthy new baby into this world." He helped Jenna stand up. "Don't worry so much! But if you feel that something is really wrong, don't hesitate to come see me, day or night."

"Okay, Doc. Thank you."

Doc escorted Jenna out the front door and then flopped onto the easy chair in the waiting room. He didn't know if anything would ever happen between him and Kat, but right now it wasn't looking good. It wasn't looking good at all.   He sighed, shook his head, and frowned.

CHAPTER FIFTY-SEVEN

MONDAY MORNING DOC woke up, shaved, got dressed, and rushed downstairs. He was glad that he wouldn't be there when Rachel showed up—he didn't need to see her right now. Hurrying to the livery, he got there in time to see Ezra hooking Crackle up to Doc's wagon.

"Thanks, Ezra! You're awesome!"

"You're welcome. What?" asked Ezra.

"Just thanks." Doc climbed into the wagon and guided Crackle down the street and left at the corner. He stopped in front of the hotel. Granny and Edward came out the door—they must have been watching for him from inside.

"Is this the getup that I have to ride in?"

"Get in, Granny, and shut pan." Edward helped Granny into the wagon, and Doc leaned over to grab her arm. Then he looked at her. "You ready?"

"As ready as I'll ever be. Now get a move on before I change my mind about this. Good-bye, dear," she said to Edward, "I'll be home before supper."

Edward blew her a kiss and looked sad.

Crackle started off slow and steady, just as Doc had

asked. Since Doc never knew when he would be toting infirm patients in the wagon, he had taught the mule to make slow starts and slow stops.

Granny, though, started moving up and down in her seat. "Can't you get that ole long ears to go any faster than that? Let's get this over with!"

"Granny, we're leaving in plenty of time. Don't worry. Just relax and let Crackle and me handle this."

"Hmmmmph." Granny folded her arms across her chest and looked at the trees going slowly by on the side of the trail.

When they turned off the main trail and headed for the cave, Granny asked, "Is this cart of yours going to fit through that cave? I don't think it is."

"It's already fit through the cave, Granny. This is the cart that Sarah carried Zack in when he was sick." They entered the cave and came out the other side. "Oh, no!"

"Now what's wrong? Do we have to go back? I hope! I hope!" Granny had a broad grin on her face.

"No, we don't have to go back, but Zack and I changed the route of the trail, and now I'm not sure we can get through. We can't. I know we can't."

"Goody!" Granny clapped her hands. "Let's go home now!"

Doc patted Granny's knee. "Don't worry, Granny, I'll figure something out."

He decided that he'd follow the old trail until the spot where he and Zack covered it over. When they got there, he turned the wagon to the left. It was high enough that it could go over many of the smaller bushes. But the going was uneven, and Granny had to grab him for balance more than once.

"Where the hell are you taking me, Doc? If you're

not careful, I'll end up in the hospital, and it will have nothing to do with my heart!"

Doc steered the wagon around a tree, and a few minutes and a few bumps later, they met the main trail. "Well, that will be convenient, Granny. While you're there, they can give you the pacemaker!"

"Not funny, Doc. Not funny."

"We're almost there."

"Doc, do you know how many times I've ridden this trail? We are *not* almost there. I'll tell *you* when we're almost there!"

"Fine, Granny, fine. You tell me." Doc had decided beforehand to go along with whatever Granny said. He wasn't going to fight her. That wouldn't help either of them.

A few minutes later, Granny pointed up ahead. "*Now* we're almost there."

Doc got out to open and close the gates, and to Doc's surprise, Granny guided Crackle through them. When they got just outside the barn, Granny showed him where to park the wagon.

"You don't need to pull out in front. I can still walk."

Doc nodded and parked. Then he unhitched Crackle and walked him into the barn. As they left the barn, Doc said, "I didn't realize you could drive a wagon, Granny."

"I was driving a wagon before—"

"Yes, yes, I know," Doc said interrupting her. "Oh, no!"

"*Now* what?"

"Zack and Madison are both at school. How are we going to get to the doctor?"

"Not to worry, Doc. See that little car over there?

That's *my* car. *I'll* drive us to the doctor."

"Now that scares me, Granny, that really scares me!"

Granny turned out to be a safe driver, though Doc had made his safety belt extra tight, just in case. The doctor's office was at the hospital—the same hospital that Kat had taken him to—which was fifteen minutes away. Granny parked, and they got out of the car and walked toward the front doors.

"Now, Doc, no offense, but let me do the talking. It's my body."

"Yes, dear," said Doc. "But you have to promise to tell the doctor the absolute truth."

Granny frowned but nodded.

CHAPTER FIFTY-EIGHT

MONDAY MORNING. DAVID and Granny had already left for Granny's appointment with Dr. Galinski. Kat shook her head and tried not to let the anger and hurt seep back into her.

After a restless night and a lot of time to think, Kat had finally calmed herself down. When she had opened that door and saw David kissing Rachel, she was devastated. And as she ran back to the hotel, she discovered that she was also livid. Incredibly livid. If she wasn't a medical professional sworn to heal, she might have gone back there to strangle him.

The nerve of him! Holding her all night long like that and then kissing Rachel. That was exactly why she had stayed away from men all these years. You couldn't trust them. Look at Billy. First he promised to love and cherish her, and then he had the nerve to go off and get himself killed. She still hadn't forgiven him for that—leaving her in the lurch like that, sixteen years old with an infant. Kat exhaled and blinked back the tears.

Time to get yourself up and face the world, she told herself. It wasn't going to get any easier by ignoring the world and lying in bed all day. Eventually, she'd have to leave the room. She exhaled sharply, got out of bed, got dressed and readied herself to go downstairs and act human. Walking briskly down the stairs as if she were full of confidence, she reached the first floor. It might fool everyone else, but right now, Kat knew that inside— inside she was a cowering little child who only wanted to sit in a corner and cry herself to sleep. She blinked that image away and walked into the restaurant.

"Good morning, Samuel. Just coffee, please."

"How are you doing today, Kat?" Samuel set the coffee in front of her.

"Can't complain. You?" Can't complain. Right, thought Kat. If you have an hour or two, I can think of one or two or a hundred things to complain about.

"Doing well, thank you."

"Is Edward around?" Kat took a sip of coffee.

"Poor Edward doesn't know what to do with himself with Granny gone. He's been scolding himself for not going with her. Now he's trying to keep himself busy by getting into trouble somewhere around here. He might be with Jenna, in her room."

"Jenna's here? I thought they weren't going to move in until tomorrow."

"She and Josiah decided that it was getting so close to her due date, that it would be better if they went ahead and started staying in town. I'll go see if I can find Edward for you."

"Thanks, Samuel." She managed to smile at him, although her heart wasn't in it. Edward was upset that he hadn't gone with Granny. Good. That would make it easier.

A few minutes later, a man entered the restaurant and

sat down. Kat had never seen him before. But since she had sent Samuel off, and she didn't hear any sounds coming from the kitchen like someone was in there, Kat decided that she needed to do something. She didn't know how to wait on him, but she could at least offer him some coffee.

She stood up and walked over to him. "Coffee, sir?"

"Yes, thank you." He continued reading a newspaper and didn't look up.

How rude, thought Kat, as she walked back to the kitchen. He didn't even look at her, like she was invisible or something. Kat realized she had been guilty of that in the past with servers, and she vowed never to act like that again. She poured the man's coffee making a conscious effort not to spill any hot coffee in his lap. Because she really wanted to.

She sat back down at her own table and sipped her coffee. Then Edward came in with an awkward smile on his face. He looked nervous—or maybe scared. That was perfect. He would be more receptive to what she had to ask of him. She hoped so.

Kat pulled out the chair next to her and beckoned Edward to sit down. Then she put her hand on top of his hand and told him what she needed him to do.

CHAPTER FIFTY-NINE

A NURSE GUIDED Granny and Doc into an examining room to wait for Dr. Galinski. Doc didn't know if Granny was nervous, but he was. He had forgotten to tell Granny not to call him Doc. Then the doctor walked in.

"Hello, Dr. Galinski. You probably don't remember me, do you?" Granny smiled up at him.

He nodded. "Oh, yes, Granny, indeed I do. I met you at a party, and when the conversation came around to high blood pressure, you told me to mind my own expletive business!"

Granny cackled with laughter and nodded. "Yep, that was me. Doctor, this is my, er, grandson, David."

Dr. Galinski shook Doc's hand. "Granny, I didn't realize you had another grandson besides Ryan."

"Oh," Granny flapped her hand at him, "my grandson-in-law, I should have said."

"I've met Jenna's husband, Josiah," he looked at Doc, "so you must be Kat's husband. I didn't realize she had gotten married again. You're a lucky man."

Doc blushed, and before he could stammer out an

answer, Granny answered for him. "Well, actually, they're not married yet, but give them some time." She grabbed Doc's hand. "But he's like a grandson to me, and that's what matters."

"Okay, well, let's see now. Kat told me something about what's going on, but let me examine you first." He took out his stethoscope, listened to Granny's heart from several different places on her chest, and nodded. "How long have you noticed the symptoms?"

Granny started to say, "Well, not—" and then Doc squeezed her hand, and she said, "At least a couple of months, and it's gotten worse lately."

"Any other symptoms?"

"Dizziness and fatigue."

The doctor nodded again, turned away, and started filling out forms while Granny waited. Doc didn't know what to say, so he looked at Granny, and she shrugged. Then Dr. Galinski turned around and handed Granny the paperwork. "You need to take some tests, so I can recommend the best treatment for you. I understand that you don't want any pills, and you *refuse* to take any invasive tests, is that right?"

Granny nodded. "Right as rain!"

"I hope a blood test isn't too invasive for you?"

Granny grunted. "I guess not."

"Okay, good. Go to the lab, and you'll get an electrocardiogram and an echocardiogram. Normally, I would insist on more tests, but Kat assured me that if I insisted you would walk right out of here."

Granny nodded again. "And I'd probably slap you on the way out!"

The doctor laughed and handed Granny the paperwork. "I probably can't get the blood work back right away, but results from the other two tests will be here when you return. I'll see you in an hour or so. Okay?"

"Okay!" said Granny, stepping off the examining table.

"Thank you, doctor," said Doc.

They walked down the hallway and into the lab. After Granny had the blood test, a nurse led her to an examining room and told her to put on a gown.

"You'll have to wait outside for this, David, but you'll want to see how it's done. When you see the technician come in, just follow."

Doc nodded, and a few minutes later, the technician walked in. Before she had a chance to close Granny's door, Doc followed her in. The woman looked at Doc and was about to say something, but Granny spoke up.

"That's my grandson. I want him here with me."

The woman nodded, had Granny move over next to a small machine, and began attaching things to her body. She attached several to Granny's chest; Doc, embarrassed, didn't look where they were attached. Then she attached one to each arm and each leg. The woman turned on the machine, and several minutes later, it stopped. "All done," said the woman. "Your doctor will have the results as soon as you return to him. Now, you need to go to the next room for your echo."

Doc followed Granny into the next room. "David, you are welcome to stay here and watch. But they're going to expose my old, wrinkly chest, and I don't know if you want to see that." Doc shook his head. He was embarrassed enough already. "But do you see that?" She pointed to an instrument attached to yet another small machine. "They will roll that over my chest and it will create a picture of my heart for the doctor. Cool, huh?"

"Awesome," said Doc, and he meant it. "But I'll wait for you out there."

Forty minutes later, Doc was beside himself with worry. The other test had finished in minutes, why was this one taking so long? Had they found something really bad with Granny's heart? Had she died on the table? No. Not that. They would have told him *that*. Finally, just when Doc had decided to knock on the door to make sure everything was okay, Granny came out with her clothes back on.

"All done. Now let's go back to the doctor and see what he says. I'm eager to get back home!"

Back in the doctor's examining room, they waited for Dr. Galinski to return. A few minutes later, he walked through the door.

"Everything checks out, Granny. Your EKG did indeed show an arrhythmia—one that would probably be taken care of with medication."

Granny shook her head vehemently. "No! I don't want to be on pills. Ever. Don't want 'em."

"Okay, then. I've scheduled you for a pacemaker insertion. The appointment is in an hour, but I may be late. I need to see two patients before then. Go back to the front desk and check yourself in. I'll see you in an hour!" The doctor started to go out the door.

"Doctor, wait! What do you mean check myself in? You mean check myself in to *the hospital?*"

"Standard procedure, Granny."

"But I'll be going home today, right?"

"That's a possibility," said Dr. Galinski, and before Granny had a chance to say anything else, he left the room.

"I don't like the sound of that," said Granny.

CHAPTER SIXTY

DOC WAITED WITH Granny in the hospital room. While they waited, Granny showed Doc all the amenities in the room, including the remote control television, the bed that moves up and down with a button, and the button to call the nurse. For Doc, it was all still amazing to him. He kept Granny talking and explaining so she wouldn't get nervous. Then the nurse came in to take her into the room where she'd have the procedure.

"Wait!" Granny held up her hand to the nurse. "Am I going to go home after this or not? Because if not, then I'm not having it done, and I'll go home right now!"

"That will be up to the doctor, ma'am." And when Granny wouldn't budge, she added, "People have gone home the same day before."

"That's more like it," said Granny, as the nurse disappeared out the door.

Doc didn't know how long the procedure would take, but considering it was the heart, he thought it might be a long time. Maybe eight or ten hours? But looking at it another way, if people could go home after having it done, maybe five or six hours? Regardless, Doc figured he had at least an hour to do what he wanted. And what he wanted was to explore every inch of the hospital—at least where he was allowed to go. The secret was to pretend that you belonged. He was grateful that he had changed into his "twenty-first-century clothes" before leaving the house. At least he fit in better. He knew there were places that Kat had taken him that he couldn't go to himself. But he would investigate all that he could.

After walking around for forty-five minutes, he found himself in the hospital chapel. It was a welcome relief from the sounds and smells of the busy hospital. He breathed deeply and relaxed. Then someone came in crying. Something caught in his stomach. Doc didn't like listening to people cry—it bothered him. That's why he had comforted Kat. But this was a stranger. He wouldn't intrude on her grief or whatever it was, so he left the chapel.

As he walked around and thoughts of Kat crossed his mind, he realized that he could cry over that. After he had held her all night long, and although she had left before saying anything to him, Doc had felt that she had accepted and appreciated his comfort. And he thought that was a big step for Kat, who liked to act so independent. Doc thought they were going somewhere—somewhere together—on an adventure of a lifetime. An adventure of love.

And then Rachel had to go and spoil everything. What rotten timing that was. She was a good friend, but what she had done was completely inappropriate. He shook his head. She ruined everything. Would Kat ever forgive him—forgive him for something that he hadn't even done, but she thought he had done? He didn't know. All he knew was that he'd have to try talking to her, explain everything. But in the end, he knew that if it was meant to be then it would happen, and if not, then it wouldn't.

He found himself back in Granny's room. It had been more than three hours. Doc sat in the chair on the far side of the bed, stretched out his legs, and tried to unwind. His eyes had started to close when a nurse brought Granny into the room. She looked groggy. Once on the bed, the nurse hooked Granny up to a new machine that he hadn't noticed before. Then the nurse was gone, and he and Granny were alone in the room. Doc didn't say anything and neither did Granny. Soon, Doc heard her snoring.

Later that afternoon, Dr. Galinski walked into the room, which woke Granny up. "Everything looks good, Granny."

"Good. That means I can go home, then." She began swinging her legs off the bed, but Dr. Galinski stopped her.

"Not so fast. No showering for five days. No golf, swimming, or bowling. You can't lift anything more than ten pounds for six weeks. You need to take it easy, although walking every day after tomorrow would be good. And you can't drive home from the hospital. If you drove over here, your grandson can drive you home."

Doc and Granny looked at each other, but didn't say anything. "So I can go home today then, right?"

Dr. Galinski exhaled. "No, Granny, sorry. I understood from Kat that you would immediately go 'back to where you came from' and be unreachable for all practical purposes. Is that correct?"

Grumbling, Granny nodded.

"Then I would prefer—insist really—that you stay a day or two to make sure that everything is working properly."

"Oh, no! I am *not* staying two days in this confounded hospital. No way! Absolutely no way!" She folded her arms and looked at him defiantly.

"All right, Granny. You drive a hard bargain. If everything checks out tomorrow morning, I can let you go then." He winked at Doc.

"Great, now that we have that settled, when can I eat? I'm starving!"

"I'll have food sent up right away, Granny."

Granny motioned toward Doc. "For my friend, here, too."

"As you wish." The doctor nodded and left the room.

"I hate that I have to stay here overnight. Edward and I have not been apart for this long since we were married. I miss him, terribly."

"You don't have to miss me anymore, you old biddy!" Edward strode in the door with a vase of red roses. "I couldn't let the love of my life spend a night in the hospital without me." He bent down and gently kissed Granny on the forehead.

"Edward! You're here!" Tears slipped silently down Granny's cheek, and Edward wiped them away. "But how'd you get here, you old coot?"

"Surprise, Granny!" Madison walked into the room carrying more flowers, followed by Zack who had a handful of magazines and an iPad.

"We brought him over for you. He couldn't stay away! We'll take your car back home, and pick you up tomorrow morning when you're ready. And we'll take Doc

244

back, so you two can be alone." Madison put the vase of flowers on the counter beneath the television.

When Doc left the room with Zack and Madison, he saw that Granny, holding Edward's hand, had a look of sheer bliss on her face.

CHAPTER SIXTY-ONE

AFTER KAT HAD returned from escorting Edward to the twenty-first century and had taken care of Paisley, she returned to the hotel. She was grateful that Madison and Zack happened to be home so they could take him to the hospital and show him where Granny's room was. She didn't want to see Doc *or* Granny right now. They had both hurt her, and she didn't need to see them and be reminded of that hurt. If Jenna weren't pregnant and about to give birth, Kat thought that she would return to the present and never give another thought to the nineteenth century or any of the people here. She was that hurt and that angry.

But Jenna *was* pregnant, and Kat had made a commitment to stay and help her. So she would—but she wasn't happy about it. But—Granny. Although she was a cantankerous old woman, Kat loved her. And it would be best to make peace with her. Doc, though, she didn't care if she ever saw him again. No, that wasn't right. She *didn't* want to see him ever again.

Kat walked into the hotel, and no one was at the front desk. She decided that after such an emotionally

246

charged day, she could use a cup of coffee, so she walked into the restaurant. Jenna was in there, seated at a table by the door.

"Hi, Kat! I'm sitting here because I have to pee every five minutes."

Kat smiled at her younger sister. "I doubt if it's that often, baby sister."

Jenna tilted her head and looked at her. "You haven't called me that for two decades."

Kat shrugged. "It seemed appropriate right now."

"I heard you took Edward to the new Red Bluff to see Granny. That was nice of you, Kat, after what Granny did to you."

Kat nodded, but didn't say anything.

"You know, Kat, Granny didn't mean that in a malicious way. But you don't understand how much it means to her to live here—in this backward, inconvenient place. Which reminds me, I have to pee again. I'll be right back."

Jenna struggled to stand up and then left the room. She returned a few minutes later.

"That was quick," said Kat.

"Ryan built a quickie composting toilet for our room. It would kill me to have to go to the outhouse every time."

"Oh, that's right!" Kat laughed. "That was part of the condition of moving in here instead of into Josiah's office."

"Kat, back to Granny. Please don't feel hurt by what she did. You know what a rebel she can be. She might not have wanted you to go just because you suggested going. She wasn't going to give in to everything. It was a huge thing for her to even agree to go to the new Red

Bluff at all. When she moved here with Edward, she swore she'd never return there."

"I guess so," said Kat sullenly.

"And I imagine you've talked to Doc by now?"

"No!" Kat said it louder than she had intended.

"Oh," said Jenna, surprised. "I thought he'd have explained to you by now."

"Explain to me what?" asked Kat, bitterly. "How he could hold me and comfort me all night and turn around and kiss Rachel the following day? I'm afraid that's an explanation I'd rather not hear."

"He didn't kiss Rachel!" Jenna sat up as straight as she could.

Kat shook her head slowly. "Don't lie to me, baby sister. I saw what I saw. How did you know about that, anyway?"

"Kat, I was in the examining room when Rachel came in—you know that chair right by the door. I *watched* what happened. I saw it all. Rachel kissed *him*."

"Well, maybe, but he didn't put up much of a fight."

"Oh, yes, he did. Doc did everything but slap her face. He was completely shocked that she had done that. He told her that they were just friends, and what she had done was inappropriate."

"Really?"

"I've no reason to lie to you, big sister. He was devastated that you had seen that. You mean a lot to him. I think that's obvious to everybody but you."

"Do you really think so?" asked Kat, brows furrowed.

Eliza walked up to the table and sat down. "So did my dad get to the hospital okay? What did he think of the twenty-first century?"

"I don't think Edward could think of anything but

seeing Granny. Madison and Zack took him to the hospital, so I just rode home."

"Kat, he was so thrilled when you offered to take him there! He didn't think he could make it a whole day without Granny!"

"I knew that Dr. Galinski would want Granny to stay overnight, so I figured I better get him over there before both of them had an apoplexy from being apart!"

The three women laughed. The door of the hotel burst open, and Samuel strode into the restaurant with a huge smile on his face, followed by Josiah with a resigned look.

"Eliza! Eliza! Look!" Samuel pointed to the deputy badge pinned to his shirt. "Josiah finally came around and made me a deputy! Come on, Josiah! Let's celebrate!"

Josiah walked past Eliza and whispered, "I'm sorry, Eliza. I had no choice." Then he followed Samuel to the back of the restaurant, where Samuel handed him a beer.

Kat watched as Eliza turned deadly pale. Her mouth dropped open, and Kat wondered for an instant if Eliza was having a stroke. Eliza put her face in her hands and said, "No, no. I can't take anymore. Ever since William and Brian died—I just can't take the loss. If anything happens to Samuel—"

"Um, Eliza," Jenna started.

"Not now, Jenna! Can't you see the woman is hurting?" Kat looked sternly at her sister.

Jenna put her hand out and touched Eliza's arm. "Eliza, I have to talk to you now."

Eliza looked up with a tear-stained face. "What is it, dear?"

"Eliza, I don't know how to say this. And I meant to tell you before, but it slipped my mind. I'm sorry. But Brian is alive."

"What? What do you mean he's alive? How could you know that?" Before Jenna could answer, Eliza's eyes brightened. "You looked it up on that thing? Is that how you know?"

Jenna nodded. "Yes, on the computer. When I looked up if Josiah would live long enough for me to fall in love with him, I also looked up William and Brian. William is gone. I'm sorry. But Brian dies in Red Bluff—a long time from now."

"You're sure?" Eliza gripped Jenna's hand.

"Yes, I'm sure."

Eliza stared off into space, nodded her head, and then jumped up and strode resolutely to the back table where Josiah and Samuel sat clinking their beers together in celebration.

CHAPTER SIXTY-TWO

DOC WAS GRATEFUL when he walked into the barn and saw that they had left Dolly saddled. He stepped over to his mule Crackle, stroked his face, and told him that he would see him in a day or two. Edward would drive Doc's wagon home with Granny when she got discharged from the hospital.

Walking Dolly outside the barn, Doc tightened the cinch and swung on. Eager to get home, he missed the new trail that he and Zack had designed. But he didn't realize it until he saw the wagon tracks. Edward shouldn't have any problem following the trail that Doc and Granny had used. Doc turned Dolly around and then headed up the wash.

He had made up his mind. He would fix the flint between him and Kat. She was going to listen to what he had to say—that there was nothing between him and Rachel, and that *she* had kissed him, *not* the other way around—even if he had to tie Kat up to do the listening. There had been no other woman that he had felt this way about, and he wasn't about to let her get away. He loved her, and he felt that if she would allow herself to

251

feel it, she loved him, too.

Doc and Dolly entered the cave on the twenty-first-century side and exited on the nineteenth-century side, and Doc was more determined than ever to make Kat understand. When he had awoken that morning, holding Kat in his arms, he knew that she was pretending to be asleep. So when he kissed her on the lips and told her she was awesome, he did it deliberately. He wanted her to think that he thought she was asleep. It may have been the coward's way out, but he had let her know, in a subtle way, what he thought of her. And then Rachel had ruined everything—which is why he had to explain it to Kat. He wasn't going to let a woman like Kat get away if he could help it.

Dolly trotted the last few yards to the livery. She was eager to get back home to her food. Doc let Ezra put her away, and without stopping at his own house, he walked straight to the hotel to find Kat. When he walked in to the restaurant, he saw Kat, Jenna, and Josiah sitting at the table nearest the door, and Eliza and Samuel in the back talking excitedly. Doc put his hand on Kat's shoulder and said, "I'd like to talk to you, Kat. I need to tell you something, and I would appreciate it if you would listen."

"Okay." She looked at him but didn't stand up.

"Over here. This is personal." Doc pulled out her chair for her.

Kat stood up, Doc put his arm through hers, and she willingly followed him a few steps away from the table. Doc put his hands on her shoulders, hoping the contact would help. "Kat, I did not kiss Rachel. She kissed me, and I was *not* a willing participant." There was some noise in the background, but Doc's entire focus was on

Kat. "I pushed her away immediately and told her that it was inappropriate. Do you understand?"

Kat nodded her head. "Yes, I believe you."

Doc took a quick step back. "You do?"

Before Kat could answer, Eliza, Samuel, Josiah, and Jenna who were holding hands in a circle, bumped into them, and grabbed Kat's and Doc's hands to join them. "We're going back east! We're going back east to find our son!" Eliza shouted.

Jenna stepped out of the circle, which made the circle more rowdy—they had controlled their enthusiasm to accommodate a very pregnant Jenna. Now the others jumped up and down, shouted, and kicked their feet. Doc heard something in the background.

"Excuse me. Excuse me," said Jenna. "I think it's time."

Doc glanced at Jenna and at the puddle of water on the floor, and he pulled Kat free.

"Jenna!" Kat said, "Your water broke!"

"I know," said Jenna. "I've been trying to tell you."

Doc and Kat, one on each side, walked Jenna to the back room where she and Josiah now stayed. Josiah reached the door before them and opened it up.

"Don't put her on the bed yet! I'll be right back!" Leaving Jenna in the care of David and Josiah, Kat ran upstairs to her room, grabbed her medical bag, and ran back downstairs while pulling something from it. After entering the room, she closed the door on Eliza and Samuel who waited just outside. "Sorry! Then she spread out a large piece of plastic on the bed and said, "Let's get her on the bed now."

Doc put his hand on Jenna's bare belly. "It's coming soon. Oh, I think it's coming now!" While looking into

Jenna's eyes, Doc put his hands out to catch the baby.

"Doc? What are you doing?" Kat stood shoulder to shoulder with him.

"I'm delivering this baby. What does it look like?"

"You aren't looking at the baby!"

"Of course not! That would be crude. I'm looking into the mother's eyes, as I'm supposed to!"

Kat shoved him over with her hip, surprising him and making him lose his balance, and she took his place in front of Jenna. "Push, Jenna, push."

Josiah knelt by the side of the bed with his arm around Jenna. "Push, sweetheart. That's good, that's good. Now breathe."

Kat said, "Thank goodness for lamaze!"

"What's lamaze?" asked Doc.

"Here it comes! Here it comes!"

"Him," said Josiah. "That's my son you're talking about. Here *he* comes."

"We'll find out in a second, Josiah. Yup, you're right! You're right! It's a boy!"

The baby cried, and for an instant, that was the only sound in the room.

CHAPTER SIXTY-THREE

As THE FIRST rays of sunlight peeked through the cur-
tains, Kat awoke in Doc's arms, and she smiled. He had
not let her go to sleep until she answered his question—
whether she would marry him or not. She had told him
that she'd sleep on it and tell him in the morning, but he
wasn't satisfied with that. Until she promised him she
would—and would move back to the old Red Bluff,
permanently—Doc kept asking. Kat hoped that he
wouldn't always be so stubborn and insistent, because
she had agreed, that yes, she would move back there, and
yes, she would marry him.

Kat had told Doc how she had felt almost healed the
other night when he held her all night long. And then
they had talked about Billy and how she was afraid to let
herself be vulnerable with a man again, because Billy
had died, and she didn't want to go through that again.
Doc said that he couldn't give her a guarantee that he
wouldn't die, but he *could* promise her that as long as he
was alive he would love her with all his heart. Kat had
snuggled deeper into his arms and told him that was
good enough for her.

And now, while Doc slept, Kat remembered what had happened the day before right after Jenna had given birth. When Jenna and the new baby had been cleaned up and presentable, Kat had opened the door and let Eliza and Samuel inside. They had been patiently waiting outside, listening to all the noise and commotion coming through the closed door. Eliza rushed to Jenna's side and held her hand, while Samuel shook Josiah's hand. Then Josiah announced the name of the baby. Milo Stone. And everyone applauded.

As Kat stood nearby, she had seen Samuel hand something to Josiah. When Josiah opened his hand to look at it, Kat saw that it was the deputy's badge. "I'm sorry, Josiah. But I can't accept this now. Eliza and I are leaving soon to find Brian. I hope you understand."

Josiah had glanced at his newborn son in Jenna's arms. "I do now, Samuel. Don't worry, I'll find someone."

Samuel nodded once and shook Josiah's hand again. Then he turned and put his arm around Eliza who was still at Jenna's bedside.

Josiah, thinking no one was watching, glanced at Jenna and the baby, shook his head slowly from side to side, and frowned. Kat had stepped up to him. "Josiah, don't worry. Someone will turn up." She wanted to tell him about Nick, but didn't want to make any promises. Then she heard someone from the front of the hotel calling out.

"Hello? Anyone here?"

She recognized the voice. "In here! Come on in!"

Nick himself had strolled into the room. His timing couldn't have been more perfect if he'd planned it. "It looks like congratulations are in order, Josiah." He shook

Josiah's hand. Glancing at Jenna, he said, "Hi, Jenna! Hi little guy!" Then he looked at Kat as if Josiah weren't even there and whispered, "It's a boy, isn't it?" When Kat nodded, Nick looked back at Josiah. "If you're needing a full-time deputy, Josiah, I'm ready to give my notice at work."

Josiah's face had broken into a huge grin, and he grabbed Nick and hugged him. "You're hired!"

Kat felt Doc stir in his sleep, and the memories from the day before faded away. She closed her eyes and willed Doc back to sleep. She hadn't felt this loved in so long, and she didn't want to give up the feeling yet. Just another hour or two—or maybe a lifetime.